Also by Jeffrey Frank

Bad Publicity

The Columnist

The Stories of Hans Christian Andersen:
A New Translation from the Danish
(with Diana Crone Frank)

TRUDY HOPEDALE

❦

Jeffrey Frank

Simon & Schuster
NEW YORK LONDON TORONTO SYDNEY

Simon & Schuster
1230 Avenue of the Americas
New York, NY 10020

This book is a work of fiction. Names, characters, places,
and incidents either are products of the author's imagination
or are used fictitiously. Any resemblance to actual events or
locales or persons, living or dead, is entirely coincidental.

Copyright © 2007 by Jeffrey Frank

First Simon & Schuster hardcover edition July 2007

SIMON & SCHUSTER and colophon are registered
trademarks of Simon & Schuster, Inc.

Designed by C. Linda Dingler

Manufactured in the United States of America

1   3   5   7   9   10   8   6   4   2

Library of Congress Cataloging-in-Publication Data
Frank, Jeffrey
Trudy Hopedale / Jeffrey Frank.
p.   cm.
1. Washington (D.C.)—Fiction. 2. Political fiction. 3. Satire. I. Title.

PS3556.R33423T78 2007
813'.54—dc2   2007000891

For information about special discounts for bulk
purchases, please contact Simon & Schuster Special Sales
at 1-800-456-6798 or business@simonandschuster.com.

ISBN-13: 978-1-4165-4924-6
ISBN-10:   1-4165-4924-2

For Diana, again,
and for
Thomas and Jody

Donald Frizzé

Washington,
the late spring of 2000

One

NOT LONG AGO, on a hot morning in late May, Trudy Hopedale telephoned, interrupting my work. She wanted me to dig up the names of famous people who had been guests in her house way back when. "I've been telling everyone that Lincoln liked to drop by," she said, with a charming giggle, "and General Patton. And that friend of Roosevelt's —I can't remember his name. Archie Butt? Could you find out for me?"

I usually try to help Trudy, because Trudy will do whatever she can to help me. Trudy and Roger Hopedale are almost the finest pair in Washington, and even though it's gotten very hard for me to work with so many interruptions, turning down a request from either Hopedale was unthinkable.

"Also, we're having a few people over for dinner tomorrow, and wondered if you were free," Trudy continued, mentioning the names of her guests, almost all of whom I knew by name.

I accepted her late invitation right away (I almost always did) and, as usual, felt mild guilt at my inability to reciprocate. The Hopedales have a grand house, on P Street near Thirty-first. I live on the west side of Wisconsin Avenue, close to the university with its complement of noisy, intoxicated students. The Hopedales have space to entertain and, I believe, five bedrooms upstairs; I have two bedrooms, one of which serves as my study, and almost no room for guests, although the downstairs leads out onto a brick patio where I can serve drinks and hors d'oeuvres if the weather cooperates, which it rarely does.

"That's so sweet of you, to take the time," she said, and hung up, seemingly unaware that I had to set aside my own research in order to consummate this favor. I stared at a red spot above my wrist, the result of being bitten that morning by a mosquito; although I tried not to worry, I was aware, as everyone was, of the outbreak of West Nile encephalitis along the East Coast. All mosquitoes looked the same, but I knew that some were potentially deadly and that my bite might be a bad one.

As I say, I usually try to do whatever I can to help the Hopedales, who, in the past three years, have come to play such an important part in my life. I had met Trudy and Roger when I set out to write a biography of Garret Augustus Hobart—William McKinley's vice president—and after I discovered that Hobart had briefly lived in the Hopedales' house, I telephoned them out of the blue and impetuously asked for a tour. Once the Hopedales got past the idea that a stranger wanted to inspect their rooms, and that some historical clue might emerge, they could not have been nicer, and our friendship sprang up almost instantaneously. I suspect that is what launched Trudy's interest in local history.

A word about Trudy Hopedale, in case there's anyone who doesn't know who she is: First, she is an attractive woman, with sleek dark hair, although parts of her body are perhaps one size too large. I'm actually not sure how old she is, but I would guess about forty-five; it's hard to tell at that age. Roger of course comes from another generation—he's at least fifteen years Trudy's senior—and there were times, during their dinner parties, when he would look wearily at his wife, as if she were an eccentric appliance and he had lost the off button. This inner energy was a trait that served Trudy well in her job as a television hostess, where she was expected to bubble, as she put it, on cue. But even off camera, Trudy was likely to bubble; that was part of her appeal. Roger of course has been in the Foreign Service for nearly forty years, and he wrote a distinguished book called *The Edge of American Power: The Paradox of Supremacy,* which few took note of, probably because dozens of other books had roughly the same title. I've begun to worry about Roger, because he told me not long ago that he's working on a novel—something made up—and I think that he wants me to read it. Although he's still officially in the Foreign Service, he stays home a lot and seems, if I'm to be honest, a little lost.

I know that when Trudy asked for her favor, I ought to have resented the intrusion; there had been far too many of them and my research in the last year or so has barely progressed. The truth, however, is that I was not entirely sorry at having an excuse to change subjects. In fact, after three years, and with deep regret,

I was close to abandoning Hobart, out of a fear that there was nothing very interesting about his life. I know that some people in our circle consider me a dilettante, possibly because of my special area of interest, the vice presidency, but I also knew that the best refutation would be my own scholarship—that is, if I could just get going.

Two

❦

I HAVE A TELEVISION career too, a modest one, and for that I do blame Trudy Hopedale. "I know you love the attention!" she says to tease me, but in fact the pleasure is fleeting and the toll it takes is significant. My commentaries may be instructive, but I doubt that anyone pays much attention to them or long remembers their content.

Trudy's People is on every day at noon, and she says that her ratings are excellent, although I've heard the opposite. Someone must have been watching, though, because about a year ago I was asked to become a historical analyst (my term) for CBS, most often for national events that require the focus, as it were, of a wide-angle eye. Because of these not infrequent appearances, all of which rob me of uncounted productive hours, I'm occasionally recognized on the street or at the Safeway. I've discovered that simple recognition—*"I've seen you someplace . . ."*—is a form of power and realize that the pleasure I derive from it is a sign of personal weakness. Trudy doesn't believe me when I say that I'm troubled by the phenomenon of cheap celebrity and she just repeats, "You love it, you love it, you love it!"

One of Trudy's charms is the skill with which she conceals herself, much like an exotic dancer. It gives her an aspect of mystery, and even when I learn something new about her, even something scurrilous, it only makes her more elusive. I hear most of the anti-Trudy gossip from people who are jealous of the Hopedales. That is quite a long list and, as Trudy sometimes reminds me, she is very particular about her circle; those who are left out tend to turn on those inside. I feel very lucky to be inside the Hopedale circle.

ALTHOUGH I'VE ONLY known Trudy and Roger for three years, their house brings back memories. It's not a historic house by Georgetown standards—it was built in 1855, for a southern senator named Pearce, whose diaries could be of inestimable help if I were ever to explore the antebellum period—and much of the structure has been subtly altered to conform to modern times. The former servants' quarters, for instance, are now home to Trudy's pale blue Mercedes SLK. The library was long ago scattered to relatives and booksellers and became the room where Roger and Trudy, who bought the house in 1984, a century after Senator Pearce's death, have installed their flat-screen television. But the living and dining rooms are relatively unchanged, and of course it is there that one finds a center of Georgetown social life.

Not, I quickly add, that Georgetown's social life is very stimulating these days. Nearly eight years with the Clintons have certainly narrowed our conversational range, and far too many dinner parties include discussions of oral sex and stained dresses, thongs, and "completion." As one witty woman remarked, all that detail is hard to take while munching on a salad covered with ranch dressing. (To that, Trudy said, "Ugh!") We've all become weary of the Clintons, and Trudy and Roger—neither of whom reads much history—blame the Clintons themselves for that. I tend to blame the age that we live in, which happens to be inhabited by people like the Clintons, and as this summer wears on, I'm sure that people will finally turn toward the future and the November election.

Yet most people don't seem really to care who gets into the White House. Roger, who knows George W. Bush and worships his father, told me that the young Bush has a "wicked sense of humor" and he wants him to win. My friend Walter Listing—if I have a tutor in this town, it's probably Walter—wants the second Bush too; he thinks that will mean another chance for him to "make a difference." (Walter had been an important intimate of President Reagan and now runs a consulting business downtown, but what he most wants is to return to his weaponry specialty at the Pentagon.) I'm not sure what Roger wants. Ambassadorships have always eluded him, but his résumé includes several foreign postings, including two in Central America, and George H. W. Bush once consulted him on tangled negotiations regarding border disputes—experiences that contributed to his thoughtful book. I don't know what ended Roger's first marriage, or what brought Roger and Trudy together, but I always intended to find out.

✤

ONE REALLY COMES to understand the Hopedales' world when Roger and Trudy have their Fourth of July barbecue, where just about everyone shows up. Members of past administrations cling to Washington like rings on the inside of a tub, and in two or three hours, it is possible to move through several decades.

Their barbecue is an elaborate production. The backyard is covered with tents and chairs and a corner of the lawn is reserved for a pit, where pork is mined in huge quantities. Elsewhere, you can find all the traditional American foods—potato and macaroni salad, coleslaw, corn, and fritters, alongside sliced turkey, ham, and fried chicken. But this list cannot suggest the elegance of the surroundings, the attentiveness of the help, or the cheerfulness of the music, supplied by retired musicians from military bands. As the light in the sky begins to fade and the band strikes up something from its repertoire of Sousa marches, Trudy and Roger lead the guests in a small parade around the grounds and one feels that something magical is occurring, even before the fireworks begin. I've been to three of these occasions, and every year I'm grateful to be part of it.

This year, though, the Hopedales have decided to skip the barbecue—the political conventions and all the rest make it too difficult—and so their essential party will not return until the summer of 2001. I don't like it when the order of things is changed, when traditions are set aside, and I suppose that partly explains the mixture of near panic and dread that's dominated my mood in recent days. A fuller explanation, though, still escapes me.

Three

✿

I T IS TIME TO SAY a little about myself, starting with my birth in 1966, in Enola, Pennsylvania, not far from the state capital, and my name, Donald Frizzé. My father was a brain surgeon (he invented the Frizzé scalpel, with its myriad applications), and his royalties, while not immense, were enough to guarantee our comfort. My mother, like myself a compulsive reader of history, always encouraged me to study and to ask questions. After the malpractice suit, my parents retired and moved to Sea Island, Georgia, and I try to visit them whenever I have the time.

I was precocious. Even in elementary school, my homework papers focused on the great issues of war, peace, and diplomacy. I attended my father's alma mater, Darleigh College, in western Massachusetts, and my faculty adviser was the eminent presidential historian G. Buster Morgenmount, whose biographies of Tyler, Lincoln, Harrison, Cleveland (two volumes), Wilson, Taft, one

Roosevelt, Eisenhower, and Ford fill the shelves of any library worthy of the name. Professor Morgenmount was a patient guide and gave invaluable advice when I struggled to finish my senior thesis—an apparently revisionist examination of the life of John Nance Garner.

Professor Morgenmount urged me to pursue an academic career in our field, and we frequently discussed my life after college. He had a habit of stopping in midsentence, as if he were trying to remember something, and then peering at me with unnerving intensity, patting my hand as I attempted a reply. His office felt small, and it seemed to shrink whenever he added books by other presidential historians, some of which (those farthest back or closest to the ceiling) were covered with moth wings and had little papers jutting out to mark forgotten citations. Over time, I came to view my professor's life and work with much admiration but little enthusiasm. While we both could become excited by burrowing into the dry documents of the past, I realized that I needed something more—the powerful odor of contemporary life—to accompany my excavations.

"I worry that you're going to disappoint me, Donald," Professor Morgenmount said not long before my graduation, as if he sensed my plan to become an independent scholar. When he made such remarks, I would get that stare of his and that pat of his hand. With his long, straight nose, tangled gray eyebrows, and the deep solemnity of his fixed gaze, G. Buster Morgenmount resembled a portrait of a nineteenth-century statesman.

Of course I didn't require a salaried position, academic or otherwise; the Frizzé scalpel gave me the sort of financial security that Professor Morgenmount would never know. But his opinion mattered to me, and now and then, as if to prepare him for my ultimate decision, I pointed out that whatever career choicc I made, I was young enough to change course and perhaps would return to campus life. At that, he nodded, stroked my wrist, and said, "I'm sure you can write popular books and find important new friends, but I fear for your serious scholarship."

When he expressed such misgivings, I assured him that I intended to be serious and that my respect for him and his work would always influence my scholarship.

THE WEEK BEFORE graduation, I informed Professor Morgenmount of my decision to become a vice presidential historian and, within this uncharted area, to chronicle the lives of truly forgotten men who were, for a time, so close to the presidency. I tried to read his baffled expression as I told him this, and I had no reply ready when he said, "For Christ's sake, Donald, who the fuck cares?"

He must have known how these words could affect my self-confidence and, furthermore, that I wouldn't argue with someone I respected so deeply. My only response, I realized, was my work, which became my complete focus. My first book, published five years ago, was of course *Benjamin Harrison's Sidekick,* a life of Vice President Levi Morton, the man who drove the first rivet into the Statue of Liberty. My Morton biography was praised in several scholarly journals, and a respected critic used the phrase "This will certainly remain the standard work for Mortonians." But it still rankles that at least one reviewer raised doubts about the originality of my scholarship. Apparently, another Levi Morton biography had appeared in the early twentieth century, but I'm almost certain that I never saw it; it's been out of print for years, and I was actually surprised to learn that copies remained extant. The coincidental overlaps of phrasing and quotation are the sort of oddity that haunts all historians. Perhaps I'm too sensitive, but it hurt that I never heard a word of encouragement from Professor Morgenmount, to whom I dedicated the book, and I suspect that he may have envied my youth, energy, and family wealth.

I'm proud of what I've accomplished, although I realize that it's come at a personal cost. I've reached the age of thirty-four with no family of my own and a life subsumed by work. I date women, of course, and Trudy and others keep trying to "fix me up," but I've yet to find someone with whom I've really clicked. My romantic life is a mystery to Trudy Hopedale (I know that she wonders about—I hate that word!—my sexuality), and I intend to keep it that way; I adore Trudy, but she loves to talk about her friends and acquaintances with fascinating indiscretion. Gossip is the gasoline of this town, and I don't intend to provide Trudy Hopedale with any fresh fuel concerning myself.

Four

THAT LITTLE DINNER at the Hopedales was no different from countless others, but by the time I got home, a
little after nine-thirty, I was already disturbed by my recollection
of the evening, as if it had been a dream in which I'd misbehaved.
There were eight of us, and not a comfortable mix: Roger and
Trudy, of course; Senator Ricardo Willingham, an overweight Re-
publican from the Midwest—he appeared to be in his fifties—who
had recently been a guest on Trudy's television program; a young
White House aide named Jeremy and his wife, who was quite
pretty but looked as if she hadn't slept in weeks; Roger's mother,
Henrietta, whom Trudy always seated between herself and Roger,
almost as if they wished to silence her (one could always sense
tension between Trudy and Henrietta); and Jennifer Pouch, a reporter for the *Washington Post* and an old friend of Trudy's. I'd
met Jennifer several times and—I know this sounds immodest—it

was fairly clear that she was interested in me. It's a pity that she's not my type, although technically she is attractive and only a few years older. I'm not a bad-looking fellow, or so I've been told; at least one newspaper article has referred to me as a "brilliant, dashing, wavy-haired historian." I enjoy these compliments, up to a point.

Sometimes dinners with Roger and Trudy were insubstantial but accompanied by enough wit and pleasantry to save the evening; sometimes the discussions were deeply thoughtful, as the men and women of our town discussed with surprising depth the events that shape our nation's purpose. But on this particular night, nothing went as it should, and now and then, when clouds of silence passed over the table and I noticed Trudy frowning (and her mother-in-law glaring, sometimes at Trudy), I tried to think of ways to rescue the occasion. Every attempt failed, and so I finally fell back on the Clintons. When I asked Jeremy, the White House aide, what he was planning to do after the election, the chubby senator interrupted and said, "He has disgraced us all, that man, with his lies and abominable behavior."

Jeremy glared at Willingham and said, "You people will do anything to destroy this president."

"Clearly not enough," the senator replied.

At this exchange, which sounded even uglier than it looks in my recording of it, Trudy seemed alarmed. Then, in her most soothing voice, she said, "I think we all need time to recover from Bill and Hillary."

"So ugly and dirty," the senator said.

"Soiled," Roger Hopedale said, as he joined this discussion.

"The Clintons have soiled our town, and we'll pay for that long after they're gone."

Washington, as any historian will tell you, is a place that is perpetually soiled, as it were. Still, my host was making the pronouncement, and so I nodded respectfully, as if agreeing.

"We can't wait to leave this dirty, soiled town," Jeremy said with an ironic sneer, and his wife, although she said nothing, looked more miserable than she had all evening.

The senator and the White House aide glared again at each other and Roger glanced nervously at Trudy. When Roger's mother said, "I think you're all jealous of Bill Clinton because he's a real man," Trudy pretended not to hear, while I tried politely to acknowledge Henrietta's modest contribution with a slow nod. When I looked over at Jennifer Pouch, I saw that she was yawning, and not very subtly, either. Jennifer's demeanor, I realized, was slightly predatory, and even more so with her mouth gaping; as she gripped a fork, I noticed that her fingernails were bitten to their ragged ends. She had brown hair streaked blond, which made her look tigerish.

"I'm much more interested in their marriage," Trudy said, but no one responded. When she asked, "Does anyone really think they still sleep together?" I saw Jennifer Pouch yawn yet again. "I guess it always comes down to Bill Clinton's penis," Trudy finally said, gaily. I laughed perhaps too loudly at that and so, to my surprise, did the exhausted-looking wife of the White House aide. But no one else said anything, and in the horrid silence (though it lasted only seconds) Jennifer Pouch smiled mischievously at me, actually more a smirk than a smile, and yawned again. I must have momentarily assumed an expression of sympathetic bore-dom, because a moment later, Jennifer winked broadly. I had hoped that this wordless exchange—the smirk, the yawn, the wink—had gone unnoticed, but Trudy misses very little; she had seen every gesture and response, and she let me know, in a quiet, fiery way, that we'd been caught in the act of insulting the hostess. That, I believe, was something that Trudy took more seriously than almost anyone. I also suspect that she saw Jennifer pinch my buttocks—a painful, unpleasant squeeze—as we headed out the front door and onto P Street.

I WAS, AS I SAID, uneasy on the way home. I read for a while, slept badly, and still felt unsettled the next morning. I sensed that Trudy, in her own mysterious way, was truly angry with me. This town, as I have suggested, is filled with men and women who in some way have offended Trudy Hopedale, and I've always tried to avoid that fate, not least because I'm genuinely fond of her. But when I called to thank her for the dinner (Trudy counted on these calls), it was hard to gauge her reaction.

"I hope you had a nice time," she said. "I really couldn't tell from where I was sitting."

"It was grand, Trudy, as always," I replied, and added that I enjoyed everyone there. "Really fun." As I spoke, I noticed that the mosquito bite on the inside of my wrist seemed to have swollen, and that it had turned into a reddish lump the size of a small grape.

"Jeremy and his mousy wife are on the outs," Trudy informed

me. "I can't swear to it, but I hear she's screwing some lobbyist."

At that, I felt a powerful and entirely inexplicable rush of jealousy, all the odder because I could barely remember the young wife. I thought of asking Trudy if she knew much about West Nile encephalitis but sensed that this was not a conversational gambit she would appreciate.

"And I never know what to do with Roger's mother. As you know, she's never liked me—she may even hate me."

"Why is that?" I blurted out.

Trudy ignored my tactless question and said, "I mean she's eighty-seven years old and her son is, like, sixty and she still treats him like a little boy."

I could hear Trudy breathing loudly and decided I ought to drop that subject.

"And of course it's always good to see Jennifer Pouch," I said, although that was not the truth. But I needed to test the subject with Trudy.

She paused at that before saying, "I always kick myself whenever I invite Jennifer. I suppose she's a good friend, but she's very duplicitous. I don't need to remind you that she has a huge crush on you."

"I doubt that," I replied, although I was sure that she had witnessed the pinch of my buttocks.

"She wants you to ask her out. Someday you'll have to tell me why you won't."

Trudy always wanted to pry things like that out of me, and I told myself that she'd have to be content with the status quo, whatever that was. I changed the subject again. "I'm terribly worried about not making enough headway on my book," I said. "It's so easy to fall behind."

"Oh, right. You always make your work sound so essential."

"Well, the evening was terrific," I said again, trying to ignore her offensive tone. "No one does dinner parties like you and Roger."

"You're right about that," she said, and in the silence that followed, I once more felt a chill.

"And Roger seemed in particularly good spirits," I added, although I could not remember anything that Roger had said or done.

"Yes," Trudy replied. "He may have been."

I WANTED TO ASSURE Trudy of my loyalty and hurried to complete the little assignment she had given me a few days before—to learn more about the heritage of her house. It took me the rest of the day at the Library of Congress, a monotonous poking into the papers of Senator Pearce, a task rescued slightly by a shared cup of coffee with my friend Walter Listing, who had been visiting an old chum in the Dirksen Building. I'm sure that my report, when I telephoned the following morning, did not satisfy Trudy, especially when I broke the news that Lincoln had never been through their front door and that the only Grant to drop by was Mary Frances, the general's sister, who was married to a diplomat named Cramer. By the time I began to name some of the other, lesser-known personages who had orbited the Pearce house, I could tell that Trudy had stopped paying attention. What was worse, I thought that I detected something unfriendly just in the way she said, "Well thanks, Donald," and hung up without waiting for my reciprocal farewell.

I stared for a moment at my silent receiver, and after I'd whispered a useless good-bye into the mouthpiece, I thought about the rest of my day. I had a cocktail party at about six, on N Street, to celebrate some staff person's twentieth year in the House, and I had tickets to the Kennedy Center for a Shaw play that a British troupe was bringing to town. I'd invited Walter Listing to accompany me, knowing how fond he was of Shaw, although perhaps it was Coward—I couldn't remember. And I needed to return to the Library, so that I could make some headway on my project, possibly Garret Augustus Hobart, although, as I've said, perhaps not.

A little after noon, I switched on my television to watch *Trudy's People,* which on this day was devoted to infidelity, one of Trudy's favorite subjects. Somehow, though, I had lost the urge to pay attention. When Trudy said to her guests, "Come on, you know just about everybody in this town is fooling around," I found myself shaking my head as I clicked the remote and tried to make the whole thing vanish.

Five

O NE DAY IN MID-JUNE, Roger invited me to lunch at his club, the first time that he'd done that, and I accepted right away. I wasn't accustomed to seeing Roger without Trudy, and of course I wondered what was on his mind.

The Sturling Club, a meandering stone building on Massachusetts Avenue with a small cemetery in the back, was not the most exclusive club in Washington, but it was the one that appealed to me, and I expected someday to join. Several Sturling members had proposed my name to the membership committee, and I was told to expect a short wait before the formal invitation came. I'm not someone who harbors social ambitions, but as a historian, I knew that the club's patrons could be of enormous value to my work, just as it helped immeasurably whenever I was asked to the White House (once so far, although not for a state occasion) or to embassy dinners or, for that matter, to the Hopedales' home.

On the day that I met Roger, I arrived early and, after checking my umbrella (rain had been forecast on what turned out to be a muggy day), I was immediately accosted by a middle-aged man with a mustache the size of a minnow who introduced himself as Royal Arsine, a name that was vaguely familiar. "We should talk sometime," this man said, squeezing my elbow, but he moved off in another direction before I could ask why. I was feeling a little uneasy by the time I greeted a former congressman who could be helpful if I were ever to tackle Gerald Ford's brief vice presidency (it could be a companion volume to Professor Morgenmount's presidential study). I then said hello to several more people, including another Washington historian who had written an outstanding, although not overdue, history of the Red Scare. I never felt that we were rivals; quite the contrary. I deeply appreciated his generous review of my Levi Morton book (he had only minor quibbles), and I think that he appreciated my generous review of his (I too quibbled; I faulted him, I think, for giving short shrift to Estes Kefauver's run for the vice presidency).

"Donald," Roger said, for he had stealthily approached from the rear and tapped my shoulder.

"Roger," I replied with enthusiasm, turning and taking his large, dry outstretched hand.

"Thanks for coming," he said. "How are things?"

I said that all was well, although my mosquito bite was still the size of a small pea and had acquired a bright red color—worrisome, although not yet quite enough to send me to a doctor. "What a nice idea, this lunch," I added, in my most cordial voice.

"We never really get to talk when I'm at your place—there's so much going on."

"One reason I wanted this tête-à-tête," he said.

We were dressed in identical costumes: dark blue summer-weight wool suits, pale blue shirts, and subdued red ties. My wingtip shoes were black and Roger's were cordovan. A stranger might even think that we were father and son. Roger's gray hair has wonderful waves, as if each strand possesses an inner energy, and the only noticeable imperfections in his outward appearance are an odd elongation of his ears, which droop unnaturally, and wide, upturned nostrils that at certain angles appear to be staring blankly like an extra set of eyes.

A tall black man with white gloves approached Roger. "Mr. Hopedale, sir," he said, bowing slightly, and then led us to a corner table, one that overlooked the cemetery. He brushed the tablecloth with a small whisk broom (was it an accident that crumbs flew at me?) and pulled out a chair for Roger. I was left to fend for myself and found that I was directly facing that Royal Arsine fellow one table away, who, I now saw, had such tiny eyes that they seemed almost an afterthought to his face.

"Well, this is very nice," I said, realizing that I was more or less repeating myself. "It's hot out there—I can't believe it's almost the Fourth of July." I paused. "Everyone misses your annual event."

Roger nodded several times and seemed to want to move beyond banality. When he finally did speak, he surprised me. "It's not going well with me and Trudy," he said finally. "Not well at all."

"Not going well?" I said, but even as I uttered my query, he continued, "And after considerable thought, it occurred to me that I should talk to people like you, friends who might know what the matter is."

I was baffled by Roger's declaration. I had no idea what "not going well" meant, and I didn't quite see how I could ask the older man to explain himself.

"Roger," I said, "I honestly can tell you that this is the first I've heard of it. The truth is," and I lowered my voice, for I could see that Royal Arsine was watching us both with placid curiosity, "that I've felt on the outs with Trudy myself in recent days, for reasons I don't understand."

"Our Trudy can be a bit cruel and moody," Roger said, with a faltering smile. "But in your case, I wouldn't worry."

I reached for a breadstick and clumsily tipped over a glass of ice water, which dribbled onto my trousers. Roger looked weary and impatient, clearly eager to get on with whatever had prompted this lunch. Yet he then began to talk about a recent uprising in a small nation he'd once visited, a matter of so little interest to me that, as he recited the names of several rebel leaders, my thoughts began to wander. For that reason, I wasn't quite paying attention when he returned to his original subject.

"I don't know what's come over her," he said. "I know you'll say this is my imagination, but I'm not imagining her guilty looks, or that she's always late getting home from the station."

"Don't you ask about her day?"

"Of course, but then she fidgets and changes the subject and talks about a 'girls' lunch' and 'shopping,' that sort of thing. She can't shop and have a girls' lunch every day. I'm starting to suspect that she's having an affair, but I can't guess with whom. Do you have any idea, Donald?"

I certainly didn't at that time, and I told him so. I attempted to imagine Trudy Hopedale flinging herself onto a stranger's bed, welcoming hateful intimacies, a mental image I was unable to wholly absorb. Roger looked so distraught that I felt wretched at having summoned my naughty Trudy vision, and I fought off an impulse to grasp his hand and squeeze it hard.

"Our Trudy is a lot of woman," Roger said, shaking his head. "I think she is only truly happy when she's in the absolute center of things. I often feel I've let her down by not going farther with my own career. I'm sort of at a dead end, you know."

"I doubt that," I replied. "History has countless examples of men who felt their careers were over and turned them around. Think of Churchill."

Roger let loose a patient smile as he studied the menu. Although he certainly knew every offering of the club, he kept looking and finally murmured, "The vegetable curry is always very nice. And the corn chowder."

After both of us had ordered club sandwiches, he shook his head several times and said, "The problem is, I'm fairly content. I have no real desire to get another posting, and I'd even take my pension if they offered it. Trudy hates that kind of talk."

Yet even as I nodded sympathetically and said, "It's not as though you haven't done your bit," I could sense the hungry rumble of ambition behind his disclaimers.

It was then that Roger bent and reached for his briefcase, lifting it and resting it on the tablecloth. It was only when he said, "I wonder if you'd take a gander at this little creative exercise of mine," that I remembered something he'd once said about an attempt to write a novel.

From the briefcase, he removed a cardboard box filled with sheets of paper. When I peeked at the title page, *Desks of Power,* I felt something close to dread; it was then that Roger, for some reason, looked over his shoulder and gave what seemed to me a perceptible shiver. "What is Arsine doing here?" he asked, as if speaking to himself. Then he leaned forward and said, "That fellow is a very bad man." Before he could add, in an urgent whisper, "Don't look at him!" I saw that Royal Arsine was grinning, perhaps at being a momentary topic of conversation, or perhaps at something I couldn't guess.

Six

FOR SEVERAL DAYS after my lunch with Roger Hope-dale, I recognized that I needed to do something about his manuscript. I had set the box on a side table in my living room, pages bursting out as if eager to be read, and I knew that if I didn't get to it pretty soon, Roger would not easily forgive me. He had been jumpy all through our lunch, and afterward, as we walked along Massachusetts Avenue looking for taxis, he told me that he regarded his work as something out of the ordinary. At one point, with something piteous in his expression, he said, "I see it as a dreadful true portrait, Donald." Yet I put it off, in part because I feared the worst, and so the box remained, taking up space far beyond its physical size. After a week or so of this, I called the author and lied to him. "I love the beginning," I said, "but I don't want to say more until I've read every word."

"That's the best news I've heard in a long time," Roger replied, pathetically. I instantly regretted raising his hopes, even though I had won a little time.

I'm not a devotee of fiction (apart, of course, from the classics; I like Hemingway's fishing stories and I've often been told that Henry Adams's *Democracy* is the best book ever written, or ever likely to be written, about Washington). When Roger told me at our lunch that John Updike and John Grisham were his two favorite authors and "you may find a bit of them in my work," I was at a loss. I'll take another volume about our Founding Fathers any day, and in any case I'm too busy to read novels—not when reality offers such fascination. With the political conventions coming in July and August, CBS would want my commentary on the vice presidential selections and, along with everything else, I needed to bone up. (If I may momentarily leap ahead, I felt a powerful biographical attraction to both Cheney and Lieberman.) My personal life, though, was going in a troubling direction.

It started when Jennifer Pouch left a message on my answering machine. "I need to tell you something," she said, a distinctly feminine construction, taunting with its mystery. I waited a day before I returned her call, and I wish that I had waited longer, because she was bursting with gossip. To judge only from the timbre of her voice, she was thrilled with what she had to tell me.

Jennifer is in many ways a fantastic woman. She is a talented reporter, very aggressive, and she almost got a Pulitzer for a series she did on spillages. Like Trudy, she seems to know just about everyone in Washington. But she made me a little nervous—I can't deny that—and at the very sound of her voice, I recalled the sharp jolt that she'd given my left buttock when she'd squeezed it. I could not imagine beginning a relationship with her, and yet that was precisely where the conversation began to head.

"Oh, Donald," she said, "while I have you, I just had a thought: would you like to go to the movies? We always have such fun together." She paused after this misstatement and mentioned a film in which a ship sinks in a storm and everyone dies. "Pick me up at work," she said, and I could not think of a good reason not to.

I'm recalling our date, if one can call it that, because it altered forever my relationship with Jennifer Pouch and, I suppose, the course of my life. I had hoped when I pulled up in front of the building on Fifteenth Street that we were simply going to amuse ourselves like old friends. Jennifer was certainly in a mildly giddy mood when she slid into the car, showing off perhaps more of her large thighs than I wanted to see, and she began at once to talk about one of those incomprehensible personnel shifts at her newspaper that people in offices like to talk about. I was barely listening as we made our way out to Bethesda, where Jennifer had made reservations at a semi-Italian restaurant, and it was not until we were having dinner that she insisted on ruining my appetite with the nasty gossip she had promised: Trudy, she said, speaking so softly that I was forced to move my face closer to hers, was having an affair, one that involved all the sordid conventions, including trysts in hotel rooms. If it hadn't been for Roger's suspicions, I would have found this almost impossible to believe, but I did believe it, and for some reason it made me feel even worse about ignoring Roger's manuscript. I hate obligations.

"With whom?" I asked.

"That's the one missing element," she replied, licking her lips. "But I'm almost positive it's Ricardo Willingham."

"It doesn't sound like Trudy," I said, but in a weak voice, as I recalled the stocky and hairy senator from the dinner party in May.

"I think it's some sort of animal attraction," Jennifer replied, and then she giggled. "Sorry," she said, but it was clear that she had enjoyed passing on the salacious news.

By then, I was in no mood to enjoy a film, and halfway through the movie, we both must have had the same thought: that there's not much joy in watching a story unfold when you know precisely what's going to happen—and especially if you know that everyone is going to drown. So after I'd fetched another bag of popcorn and we'd polished off half of it (Jennifer chewed too loudly, *smack-smack*), we left before the onscreen storm had done its worst.

Leaving was a relief to me, and as we walked outside, where the evening's humidity had thickened, I thought that this augured an early night—that after I dropped Jennifer off, I would have time to do a little preconvention reading and might even stay up to watch *Nightline*. There was a comfortable silence inside my car as we drove south on Wisconsin Avenue, broken only when I tuned the radio to a classical station and Jennifer said, "You have to wonder about making a living as a fisherman."

I nodded, not knowing quite what to say.

"I mean, they have to get up before dawn, and sometimes it's cold and foggy—and then you get a storm like in the movie, and you die a horrible death. You go down with the fish."

"Of course we didn't actually stay, so we can't be sure they all died," I said.

"Ha-ha," she replied, and it was nice to share a laugh as we made our way safely around Chevy Chase Circle and entered the District.

A moment that I feared came as we approached her building, which hovered on upper Connecticut Avenue, and stopped in front of it. We were in an especially dark patch of the thoroughfare, and in the dim light she probably did not see my grimace.

"Why don't you come up, and we can have a cup of tea before we call it a night?" she suggested, and I believe we both knew full well what that might set in motion. "I have lots of very fine tea— Earl Grey and Darjeeling and everything."

That was not what I wanted; she was not, I'll repeat, my type. I said, "I'd love to, Jennifer, but I'm afraid it's quite late, and I have to be at the Library early tomorrow."

"Garret Augustus Hobart?" she asked, turning to me. The faint illumination from a nearby streetlight gave her that sly, slightly predatory look she sometimes gets, one that suggests she knows more than she does and that she's someone who is accustomed to getting her way. Even in the dark, I could see the tigerlike stripes in her hair.

"Exactly," I said, smiling, realizing that the words "Garret Augustus Hobart" might sound a little odd in this context. "It's true that I'm beginning to have my doubts, but old Garret won't let me go quite yet."

"So I gather."

Her lips moved closer to mine and parted slightly. I saw the tip of her tongue and realized I was wordlessly being set up for a kiss.

I felt surrounded by a cloud of perfume, but I was determined to avoid further entanglement. Of course, the male in me wanted nothing more than to follow Jennifer up to her apartment and pursue the inevitable: we would disrobe and, after some heated preliminaries, have sexual intercourse. The act itself would have gone well—the sliding in and out until she seemed content—yet if that happened, Jennifer would talk about it to others, and possibly spare no detail about my performance. So much for privacy! I know what a small town we live in, and how quickly word of one's behavior gets about. And no one in this town talks more than Jennifer Pouch.

"I have this feeling that you don't like me as a woman," Jennifer said, in a quiet voice.

I gripped her shoulder and looked at her intently.

"I think you're wonderful as a woman," I said. "But the last thing I want to do is start something that won't make both of us happy."

"Donald," she said, and in the dim light I again detected that slightly rapacious expression, "it would make me very happy if you'd come up and have a cup of tea—nothing more. After all, we've hardly talked."

At that, her lips touched mine and her tongue licked the inside of my upper lip. I didn't want to be rude, but I drew back, thinking how chilly and toothy her mouth felt.

I realized that this was getting awkward, and I had no real excuse; after all, I was a man in his thirties, and saying that I had to be at the Library early the next day to continue my research into the life of the obscure Hobart sounded strained and perhaps even dishonest.

"I could also offer you a chocolate chip cookie," she said, and then added, far too suggestively, "or perhaps another yummy sweet."

I felt around in my pocket to find change for the parking meter and invested in thirty minutes. I worried that if I put in enough quarters for an hour or more, that might seem presumptuous, and I followed her into the elevator and looked all around during the slow ride to the fourth floor.

Her apartment was much what I'd expected: Crate and Barrel furniture, framed reproductions, and books collected during undergraduate years (in Jennifer Pouch's case, at Smith, which began with art history and ended with political science). As I pretended to admire something or other, she stood behind me and massaged my neck with her surprisingly large hands. "You're a beautiful man," she said, and I thought about how often I'd heard those words from women I barely knew—fans who wrote to me after one of my television appearances.

"But I should be off," I said. "I really do have to bone up."

To that she chuckled wickedly, made an off-color pun, and said, "Don't be in such a hurry."

Some details of what happened next during this brief visit—I'm thinking now of the intimate touching and the rage—grew only more vivid in my delayed, embarrassed recollections; even months later, a gesture or movement from that evening might leap into my thoughts, and it happens still. At the time, though, I was struck by the awkwardness of it all. Almost from the moment I sat down on her curved gray sofa, sipping chilled white wine (it turned out that her tea was used up), noticing that her blouse suddenly had come unbuttoned and that her skirt had disappeared, I felt immensely sad at the weakness of the human race, its perpetual pursuit of friction and satiation. She seemed annoyed when we'd finished our beverages and I carefully checked my pocket watch. When I told her that little more than eleven minutes remained before the parking meter turned red, she looked at first perplexed. When she suddenly stood and said in a loud and angry voice, "Well, you certainly don't want to be late for your meter!" it was as if she had read my mind.

Seven

WHENEVER I SUCCUMB to the distractions of our town, they affect my work. No one wants to hear about my private indexing techniques or about the exciting discovery of a diary entry from a century ago. Rather, they want to learn about my personal life. For instance, just the other day Trudy insisted on talking about my so-called date with Jennifer Pouch. I wished now that we'd never gone out, or that after the storm-and-drowning movie I had simply deposited her in front of her building. And then I wished I had responded in kind when she'd called me a beautiful man—after all, it would not have been much of an effort to call her a beautiful woman, even if I didn't much care for her big feet, loud popcorn munching, and somewhat sloppy look. And perhaps because my vocation leads me into the past, I tend to forget how easily a modern woman may surrender the sensual favor that poets and historians once dwelled upon. Yet I turned down this primeval gratification, if in fact the prize was being offered, for reasons that are possibly inexplicable, even to me.

"I hear it didn't go so well with Jennifer," Trudy said, in that way she had of getting you to talk.

"Who told you that?" I asked, a little stupidly.

"You told her you were tired? That doesn't sound like you, Donald. And I hear you said you were going to work on that vice president you told me you were losing interest in."

I was almost ready to tell Trudy what Jennifer had said about *her*, though part of me couldn't quite believe it. Trudy and Roger had always seemed inseparable and loyal to one another.

"I *was* tired, but I can't deny there was more to it than that," I said.

Trudy's laugh ended abruptly in an unattractive snort.

"Jennifer is much older than you, maybe five years, even if she doesn't look it," Trudy said. "I'm very fond of her—she's a dear, sweet friend—but there *is* something a little too eager about her. She talks about you as if she wants to eat you up."

I kept my silence, because I didn't want to sound mean. But no doubt that rapacious eagerness was part of what stopped me from reciprocating—that and a wish to keep my private life private. I'm fairly sure that's it, anyway.

"But Jennifer was very hurt—something must have happened to hurt her feelings," Trudy was saying just when I thought we had covered the subject. "Maybe you weren't tactful?"

"I can't imagine."

"She says you—oh, I can't say it!" Trudy said.

"Say it," I commanded her.

"Well, I think she found your total lack of interest a little hurtful, but mainly peculiar."

"I was trying to be honest."

"So she wonders about you, you know?" Trudy said, in a softer voice, persisting in her clever interrogation, and to that I had no reply.

LIFE, I LONG AGO DISCOVERED, is like history: it has a way of repeating itself and of not going smoothly. I thought about that one morning when I left my little house and spotted someone half sitting on a fire hydrant across the street, checking something that seemed to have gotten lodged in the sole of his right shoe. It took me a moment to recognize the unpleasant man who had introduced himself to me at the Sturling Club and had so rattled Roger Hopedale. In daylight, I could more clearly see the lines in his face, the weariness around his minuscule eyes, and the gray in his hair. Any remaining youthfulness was washed away by the summer sun. He came toward me with an odd, half-formed smile that made his tiny mustache wiggle. "We met a while back," he said, holding out a hand to shake one of mine. "Royal Arsine," he added, as if to jog a memory that didn't require jogging.

I nodded and must have looked apprehensive, perhaps because after my lunch with Roger, I had learned a little something about him.

"Do you have time for a chat?" he asked.

I shrugged, and soon enough we were walking side by side, although not chatting. Of course I had nothing to say to him, but he nevertheless stayed alongside as I reached Wisconsin Avenue, where I looked for a taxi—feeling in a rush to get to the Library of Congress. The day was already hot, and pedestrians, with sun flashing off their dark glasses, seemed barely to move. I wore a seersucker sports coat and light khakis. Arsine wore a dark suit but unlike me did not seem to be bothered by the heat.

"Hope you don't mind my company," he said. "I can sometimes be amusing." After a moment's pause, he added, "And of course sometimes not."

I knew that there was no escape until he'd said whatever it was he'd come to say, but I was determined not to reveal my impatience. "What is it you do again?" I asked, and he looked at me strangely.

My research on the Web had informed me that Arsine had once been a "cultural specialist" in Central America but had been speedily recalled after one of those incidents that, by tradition, are kept under many wraps and insistent denials. I wanted to hurry my pace, but it was too hot for speed, and after a few minutes I stopped at a discount shoe store (we had reached N Street), and when I stared into the window I saw Arsine's reflection close to mine. As I regarded our faces and the Timberlands and Rockports and piles of sneakers, it was hard to imagine that this was the same person quoted by newspaper columnists and described by one as a man "preternaturally attuned" to the nuances of secret diplomacy.

"I could use some shoes," he said. "If you're going in."

I was feeling increasingly uncomfortable, and not only from the moist heat. Arsine, it was clear when he finally began to speak, knew a lot about me, from the Frizzé family's wealth to my long-standing friendship with Walter Listing to the sluggish pace of my Hobart biography and more. As he let me know what he knew, two of my fingers began to vibrate, and they kept up the pace when Arsine chuckled and said, "It's not hard to find out about a person."

"I imagine not," I said with an unruffled nod.

On M Street, as we walked east, we passed a group of black teenagers who seemed to find something funny at the sight of us, perhaps at my increasingly futile attempts to snare a passing taxi-cab. A moment later, Arsine said, "Listen, Donald, let me get to the point: I need you to give me Roger Hopedale's manuscript."

I was baffled by this request and annoyed by the circuitous way he had of speaking.

"Actually," he added, "you need to do this because there may be a security issue."

"You're not serious," I replied, although I could see that he appeared to be.

We stared at one another, and I was struck again by his eyes, like pricks of darkness on his pale face.

"We are serious," he said, introducing the plural pronoun. "We're not saying he did it on purpose—these slips happen all the time—but he's written something that didn't get clearance."

The day had suddenly become blisteringly hot, and I wiped my forehead with a sleeve. Arsine still appeared unaffected by the temperature.

"Why would it need clearance?" I asked.

"Don't be naïve," Arsine said, and not so pleasantly, either.

We continued—now we were crossing Pennsylvania Avenue at its complicated intersection with M Street—and I tried to think of something to say. I was not about to violate Roger's confidence, but the man walking beside me had definitely managed to unnerve me.

"A copy is okay," Arsine said. "Just go to Kinko's—we'll pay. Roger will never know."

Of course I couldn't do that; I felt guilty enough at not having actually read it. In fact, this conversation reminded me that I owed Roger another round of encouragement. ("You've done something amazing, Roger, but I need more time to gather my thoughts," I'd said the last time I'd called, and the time before that, "It would be wrong of me to rush my opinion—not when you've put so much into your fascinating work.") I had a pretty good repertoire of soothing comments, some of which I had deployed on other occasions with other people.

"Let me say this, Don," Arsine said, as if he knew that I disliked the diminutive. "As you might imagine, we know more about you than you'd like anyone to know."

When he said that, I stopped abruptly, although we were in the middle of the street and cars were heading our way, not all of them, I suspected, prepared to stop. I rushed to the sidewalk. I was about to ask if he was threatening me, but thought better of it, in part because I could not meet his tiny eyes and in part because I did not want to raise the subject. But when he said, "Maybe we could talk about *Benjamin Harrison's Sidekick,* just like two American historians walking into a bar," the implication was clear: he would not hesitate to discredit my early work and, thus, me. That worried me—I can't deny it—but it also made me angry. I would have expressed my fury, but when I looked his way again, he had somehow managed to make himself disappear behind the steamy tangle of passing cars, and a moment later I leaped, as it were, into an unoccupied taxicab, half expecting to find Arsine in the seat next to mine.

Eight

❦

I WAS NONPLUSSED when Roger's mother telephoned one morning in September (I was still shaving) and said, "Mr. Frizzé, I want to pick your brain." I loathe that phrase, which calls to mind concrete imagery and my father's surgical innovation. But it meant a welcome change of subject, or so I thought. For much of the past month, my days and nights had been filled with thoughts of Cheney and Lieberman, although I can't recall much of what I said about either one apart from passing on Walter Listing's observation (without attribution) that Cheney has always been a capable fellow, from the day he arrived in our town as a congressman. For that matter, I can barely remember being in Philadelphia or Los Angeles, although I must have been in both cities because people saw me on television and I'm almost certain that I sounded informed; Trudy sent me an e-mail saying I was "*so* brilliant" and I heard much the same thing when I attended parties night after night. I suspect that I had too much to drink on some of those occasions, and one night I woke up in a hotel room that was not my own in bed with a person I'd never met. But my employers at CBS said that they were grateful for my running commentary and they will want me to return to the booth in October, for the vice presidential debate. I'm sure that Professor Morgenmount considers this a trivialization of my field, and I wonder if he even bothered to watch me. I fear that he wouldn't tell me if he had.

I HAD OF COURSE met Roger's mother at several Hopedale dinners (although, as I may have said, Trudy always tried to seat her far from anyone but Roger and herself), but had never encountered her alone. She proposed meeting at a bistro close to her apartment in Foggy Bottom, and I hurried to be there early, reluctant to keep an old woman waiting. When I arrived, I was sorry to see that she was already seated, which left me no time to study the menu or to see who else was around. The whole thing made me uneasy, in large part because of Trudy's hostility toward her mother-in-law; I had to wonder if she would view this lunch as an act of disloyalty, but couldn't quite imagine how. Henrietta Hopedale was once considered very beautiful, but age has a way of taking charge of one's features, such as her beaked nose, which ascends slightly at its tip so that her nostrils, like her son's, sometimes resemble eyelets. (This physical trait is less noticeable on a man's face.) Her hair, which ought to be gray at the age of eighty-seven, is dark, although it has a few white strands, as if to make a down payment on the decades. She looked, I thought when I first saw her, almost angry, and while I was pulling out my chair, she asked, "Why does she have to be so mean to him?" almost as if I had interrupted a conversation that had begun without me.

"Hello, Mrs. Hopedale," I replied, tentatively and pleasantly, but before I could manage another word, she continued with what was clearly a harangue against her daughter-in-law. "Don't attempt to deny it! It's as clear as can be. And I suppose you've heard she's carrying on with that senator—the fat one with the thick lips and the Mexican name?"

Roger's mother could only have been referring to Ricardo Willingham, and I was surprised at how far the ugly rumors had spread.

"I can't tell you anything about that," I said, which was the absolute truth. I added, "You seem upset."

"Roger has given her everything," Henrietta continued, waving away a waiter who was starting to hover. "She's gotten social status, money, the wherewithal to make the splash she wants. Well, we all make bargains and I suppose Roger is no great prize when you get right down to the basics. But she shouldn't be fucking the guests."

I was startled to hear this language, and it must have shown in my expression.

"I can see you're shocked," she said.

"Not at all."

"I suppose you expected a little chitchat first—a little how-are-you and isn't-the-weather-nasty and all that," Henrietta said. "But the weather is always nasty and I'm very protective of my son. He's the sort of man people take advantage of. He's kindly and thoughtful, not like Trudy." She paused, leaned toward me, and whispered, "Trudy is Jewish."

I waited for her to go on, but that was the moment that the waiter chose to swoop down and insist that we learn about the specials, in particular the swordfish and the fettuccine. "The omelet is very nice here, and the vegetable medley," I heard myself telling Henrietta when the waiter had retreated, not knowing what had led me to make suggestions about a menu I'd never seen. But then, following Henrietta's lead, I ordered sparingly. I tried not to look at her too closely, especially when she raised her chin slightly and stared at me, as it were, with the orifices of her nose.

"On her father's side," she added. "Her mother taught school. In Detroit—the urban part, if you know what I mean."

"Lots of people teach and are Jewish," I said, when it appeared that a response was required, although this ethnic fact actually interested me, perhaps because Trudy had never told me very much about her background.

"She doesn't want people to know. But she's Jewish and she's fucking the dinner guests."

"As I said, I can't add anything to that," I replied, and I no longer entertained any doubts that she disliked her daughter-in-law.

Henrietta looked distracted, and she wrestled with a tough piece of bread for a few seconds, breaking off a ragged chunk and giving up when she made no headway with her teeth. I glanced at my wrist, where my alarming mosquito bite had thankfully faded to a small pink spot, requiring no medical attention. Then she asked, "What did you think of my son's novel?"

I wasn't prepared for that, either, and so I said, "It starts wonderfully, but I'm not yet done with the last chapters," thinking, as I said this, that I was overdue in giving Roger another call.

"He won't show it to me. I think something about it embarrasses him. I'd hate to think Roger was trying to write dirty—is there a lot of that?"

I shook my head and put my finger to my lips. I knew that my discretion impressed her and thought that perhaps this had been some kind of test. I looked around the restaurant, which was getting noisier, and saw a number of people I knew or ought to know among the diners, including, to my dismay, Jennifer Pouch, who was four tables away. She was with someone high up in Clinton's Treasury Department and was leaning toward him in a confidential posture. I recalled our one kiss and the collision of our teeth. It might have been my imagination, but I think she sent me a contemptuous glance.

"You weren't listening," Henrietta said, which was true enough; I had just missed hearing something that she clearly thought was important.

"Forgive me."

"I want to talk about Harry," she said.

It took me several moments to realize that she had been talking about President Truman, and that she was making an extraordinary claim: that they had once had a liaison which had never been hinted at by any of my predecessors in the history game.

"I've decided to tell someone and I've chosen you," she said, and looked at me with such a combination of excitement and embarrassment that I had to turn away.

"I appreciate that," I said, and although I gave her what I believe is my most winning look—a combination of large smile and empathic stare—I think that she sensed my immediate doubts.

"I've never said a word to anyone," she continued, and as the waiter set down our unappetizing lunch, I repeated to myself a favorite saying of G. Buster Morgenmount's: The preposterous is always possible.

As Henrietta explained it, she had met Truman because her husband, Thrall (a family name), had been a protégé of Dean Acheson's. I had seen photographs of the family and remembered thinking that Thrall Hopedale looked like a version of Roger, although with an improved nose.

"Harry was very shy, even though he had this reputation for being bold," Henrietta said, sipping ice water. "Thrall and I were at a state dinner for some European leader—I can't remember who— but Harry came over and asked me to dance when the Marine Band started playing. I think it was 'Stars Fell on Alabama' or maybe 'Tuxedo Junction'—that was the era. His mouth came right to my ear, you know, because he was such a short man, and two weeks later, he invited me to the West Wing for brandy."

Henrietta was short of breath, and I looked at her closely to try to gauge if she was having sport with me because I was a student of the vice presidency.

"Of course I would hate for this to get back to Harry's living relatives," Henrietta continued, "or Bess's—I know he really cared for her. But I am an old woman and why should I be afraid of the truth?"

In college, I had spent a fair amount of time on the Truman era; it was a period left uncharted by Professor Morgenmount, and I had once considered undertaking a biography of his vice president, Alben Barkley. But I'd never heard of Truman straying, so this admission struck me as ludicrous, and although I tried to look interested when Henrietta said, "Harry had a much easier time dropping that bomb on the Japs than he did hopping into bed with me," my mind wandered again.

I noticed that Jennifer Pouch was staring. Now and then, the smallness of our town gets to me, and never so much as when I'm eating a meal in an enclosed space surrounded by people I don't want to see. Henrietta too looked at me intently and asked straight out if I believed her. I had no choice but to say what G. Buster Morgenmount would have said: "I wonder if you have a letter of some sort, or a gift perhaps?" I took a sip of water and added, "Of course I don't doubt you, but I have to approach this as a scholar, not just a friend. You see what I mean?"

"You don't believe me," she said, and lowered her head. "Why would I have kept a souvenir? What if Thrall had discovered it?"

"I do believe you, Mrs. Hopedale," I said. "But—" My sentence stopped. "I also worry about your reputation."

As I thought how astonishing it would be to find something to change our view of the decisive little Missourian, Henrietta shook her head, as if she sensed a wall of disbelief being erected between us.

"You've lost all respect for me," she said, in a voice surprisingly meek.

A human shadow fell across the food that we had ordered—my cup of lukewarm vegetable soup and Henrietta's scoop of orange tuna fish—and when I looked up, I saw its origin: Jennifer Pouch.

"I had to stop by and say hello," she said, with a giant smile, and I saw that the streaks in her hair had become more sharply defined. She nodded to Henrietta and said, "Hello, Mrs. Hopedale. Do you remember me?"

"I'm not dotty," she replied, and Jennifer flinched a little at the fierce tone. "I know your byline too," Henrietta added, though not in a nice way.

I had hoped to remain friends with Jennifer despite our fizzled date. Trudy had sometimes described Jennifer as bright and energetic, but today I sensed, again, a viraginous impulse beneath the charming surface, and on some level she simply frightened me.

"Donald and I are discussing history," Henrietta said.

"He's such a sweet man," Jennifer said, and pinched my cheek, squeezing until it hurt. "A man's man," she added, giving me a horrible wink.

When she'd gone back to her lunch companion, probably a source she was draining of all information, Henrietta leaned across our table and said, "I don't think she likes you very much, Donald."

Nine

I BELIEVE THAT ROGER Hopedale understood my delays
with his manuscript—he probably watched my commentaries
during the two political conventions and had to know how busy I
was. But by mid-September I had no plausible excuses left, and
after my lunch with his mother, I finally managed to make my way
through a major chunk of *Desks of Power.*

I know that I ought to have been more curious, especially
after that strange Arsine fellow spoke to me in that menacing
way. But it's hard for me to focus on very much these days, perhaps because, like Trudy and everyone, I'm waiting for this
boring election to be over and I've run out of things to say about
it. The sad truth is that I waste too much time with useless diversions, such as when I turn on the radio and listen to people like
Bucky Ravenschlag. Bucky, as everyone calls him, fascinates me.
Maybe that's because he is so young—younger than me by

several years—or because his program has more than four million listeners and nobody I know has ever met him. Or maybe
it's because he's in a wheelchair, although no one knows quite
why; he claims to have lost strength, though not feeling, in every
part of his body but his mouth, but that may be a joke on his
part. Trudy likes listening to Bucky because he's always talking
about the Clintons, especially Mrs. Clinton, but that's Trudy for
you. I'm amazed at how happy Bucky sounds when he talks
about fighting countries that annoy him and how fond he is of
weaponry (he claims to collect Lugars and old Colts, but also
swords, spears, crossbows, and clubs). I know I shouldn't waste
my time like that, and maybe the fact that I'm not getting anything of my own done should worry me. But if I can't find time
to work, I shouldn't find time to worry, either.

In any event, I did finally plunge into Roger's manuscript, and
at almost the instant I put it down, I felt a powerful urge to toss it
into the green Supercan, which beckons so invitingly from behind
my house. Roger, I could see at once, had a talent for this sort of
thing—the Washington thriller—but not quite enough of it. I tried
to think of what to say when I telephoned, and, as if to prompt
myself, I forced myself to reread his first few hundred words:

> Senator Mitch MacPeters glanced at the note from his
> administrative aide. He had expected bad news, but not
> this: the emergence of a formidable opponent in the fall,
> a man who had been a quarterback for the Green Bay
> Packers and blamed him for not opposing the disposal of
> toxic chemicals in their state.

MacPeters scratched his ear and tapped his desk, which once belonged to Henry Clay or Daniel Webster, and stared out the window of his office, with its dun-colored walls and wainscoting of burled walnut and its floor of polished oak, at the chalky white phallic Monument. His thoughts were interrupted by a sharp knock and a soft voice that said, simply, "Senator."

When he looked up, he saw his administrative assistant, Tammy Roberts, who had forgotten to button the top of her creamy blouse. "Sorry to interrupt." She smiled.

MacPeters welcomed this intrusion. Although Tammy had worked for him for six years, and was always there, he pretended not to notice her silky skin, tanned in the summer, pale in winter, and covered with light brown freckles in the off-season. He couldn't help observing that her breasts were upright and yet she knew almost more than he did about the projection of American power in the post–Cold War world.

"The White House called ten times," she informed him in a tense voice. When she bent to adjust a stocking and exposed more of her soft self, MacPeters tried to look away, but did not succeed.

MacPeters knew what this was about: The president was still pressuring him to vote to confirm Tony Snike, a man so devious that MacPeters wondered how Snike had managed to stay out of prison. He thought of the lives Snike had destroyed—about Snike's work as an intelligence agent in Central America, and his raw, cruel, almost joyous brutality, which MacPeters had witnessed firsthand during his own short but distinguished career in the diplomatic corps. The president was determined to make Snike his new intelligence chief and was not above using any tactic to get his way. Tammy stood as if awaiting an order, and MacPeters noticed a faint blush on her downy cheeks.

"Senator, you look so worried!"

"Not really," he assured her, and he wondered why she didn't leave when their conversation was so clearly finished. Perhaps she wanted to discuss the appropriations bill?

"I . . . " She hesitated.

"You?"

"I . . . ," she repeated. When she rushed from his large, woody office, her face was pink and swollen.

As MacPeters shook his head, his desktop telephone rang. Only a few people had this number: one was his wife, Tootsie, who always seemed more interested in her endless dinner parties and social ambitions than in his welfare; another was his mother, who had recently shown more than a few signs of derangement; and then there were his major campaign donors. Even the president did not have this number, MacPeters thought, with a mental chuckle.

"Hello."

He did not recognize the voice but knew at once that the person on the other end was no friend.

"MacPeters," the voice said, huskily.

"*Senator* MacPeters," he replied, frostily, and started to replace the receiver.

"Don't hang up!" the caller said, almost as if he were able to watch him. "Just walk over to the closet and tell me what you see."

MacPeters did not have time for practical jokes. Who, he asked himself, would have this number? It had to be either someone he knew or someone to whom he was beholden. That was the way of this city, his town, where camaraderie was a contact sport.

He turned the fine brass doorknob affixed to the door of the closet. He saw his summer raincoat and winter topcoat and the rough suede jacket he used when he campaigned in the semirural parts of his state. His dinner jacket hung off to the side. Then he saw something unexpected on the floor next to a pair of patent leather shoes, hiking boots, and galoshes. At first, he thought a suit had fallen from a hanger, but he couldn't remember owning a brown suit with broad white stripes. Then he saw that the suit was worn by a corpse.

The body had been arranged so that the knife stuck straight up from its back like an angry flower. It was one of those carving knives the senator favored, because their sharp, serrated edges were so good for both bread and tough meat. "Jesus!" he breathed. Should he call the Capitol Police or someone else? Or should he summon Tammy Roberts? As MacPeters considered these choices,

57

he looked more closely at the dead man and realized that it was someone he knew: the man they had called The Interrogator when he had worked so closely, and so enthusiastically, with Tony Snike, back when . . .

That's when I stopped reading, returned the pages to their cardboard box, and tried again to gather my thoughts. I'm not proud of my talent for flattery, but once, when Trudy was annoyed with me over something, she actually said that I was "too ingratiating," and I had to admit, at least to myself, that she might be right. Then I did something I almost never did so early in the day: I mixed a tall glass of gin and vermouth, after which I telephoned the Hopedale home.

"Roger, I know it has been unforgivably long," I said, beginning our conversation, "but I had to call as soon as I was done and tell you how wonderful your novel is."

I heard him swallow before he said, "Donald, I can't tell you how much your opinion means to me." Then he coughed slightly and added, "But you took so long to finish. I was beginning to worry. I worry still."

I realized that my delays had been a torture, but it's difficult to construct a well-made lie, and I wanted to say it just right. I said, "Well, you needn't have worried. It's just a grand story, and it's clear that you have natural gifts."

"Well, thank you, Donald, but to tell you the truth, I fear that you're just being kind to an elderly fool."

I shook my head so hard that I worried about my brain and

said, "Don't be silly—I can assure you that I'm being completely truthful. Otherwise, what's the point? Of course, I'm no literary critic; I'm a historian. But I can tell you, I found it fascinating." I paused and added, "You certainly know your territory. I mean, we're a long way from Henry Adams and *his* wonderful book."

I could hear Roger swallow again, as if he'd identified a speck of doubt in my otherwise enthusiastic response.

"You said something about my 'natural gifts' just a moment ago, and I wonder if you'd care to elaborate."

Had I said that? I probably had. Words sometimes just tumbled past my lips and into the world. It's a habit I've never been able to break, particularly when I'm on television.

"Well," I said, trying to think of the apt phrase, "you have the gift of engaging a reader, which I suspect is far rarer than people believe." I paused, trying to remember the name of one or two of his characters. I wished that I had managed to get through more of it. "There was something appealing about your senator," I said, "but also something tragic."

"Yes," Roger said. "You saw that—and you saw that I wanted to do more than just tell a whopping good story?"

I nodded rapidly, eager to finish our conversation before I botched my end of it, and said, "So I just wanted to call as soon as I was done."

"You thought it was a whale of a yarn?" he asked, and I tried to remember if I'd said that too.

"Oh yes," I replied. The more we talked, the more I realized that I hadn't paid attention even to what I thought I'd read. Roger had spent countless hours producing his novel, yet I hadn't found the time to read so much as a single line with much attention. The unfairness of this shamed me, and I realized that I would have to read more of it before we spoke again.

"Do you think," Roger asked, "that I will be able to find a publisher?"

"Oh, I think so," I said, praying that this would close down the subject. I tapped his manuscript, a sheet of which spilled over its cardboard partition. I reached to tuck it back in.

"We really should lunch again," Roger said, in a voice that sounded a little distant. "I'd love to hear more about your own work. I've been so caught up in my project and not even asked—selfish of me."

For the first time, I had a mournful premonition about the Hopedale family. I feared for Roger's reaction to the inevitable fate of his novel, and I feared for the stability of his mother, whose fantasy about Truman seemed all too real to her. Then there was Trudy. The last time I had appeared on her program, she looked tense in a way I hadn't seen before, on the cusp of old-womanhood. That had nothing to do with her age but with an odd flicker of defeat in her eyes—so unlike the Trudy I had come to know during the last three years. And I worried about that odd Royal Arsine and the mischief he seemed eager to unleash.

"Are you still there, Donald?" Roger said, and I realized that I had more or less forgotten that we were talking. "For a moment I thought you'd hung up without saying good-bye."

We did say good-bye then, after he'd spoken once more of

another meal at the Sturling Club. I worried, not for the first time, that the personal demands of this town were overwhelming me. Guiltily, I picked up Roger's manuscript, carried it to my coat closet, and placed it on the floor, next to the umbrellas, some of which had nested there for years like little porcupines.

Ten

P ERHAPS IT'S THE EARLY fall heat, but I've more
or less decided, with absolute finality, to set aside my
Hobart project. Although a manuscript does not quite exist, I
say "set aside" in the sense that I'm unlikely ever to return to
this misbegotten venture. No one I know has ever heard of
Hobart and no one appears to have the slightest interest in
learning anything about him, although his life does suggest a
fascinating "what if" scenario. (If Hobart had not died at the
age of fifty-five, he likely would have run for a second term
with William McKinley, in which case, Garret Augustus
Hobart, not Theodore Roosevelt, would have become president when McKinley was mortally wounded in Buffalo.) But
none of that happened, and the truth is that I have grown
bored with the subject. This whole historian business has me a
little bored, to tell the truth, and perhaps it always has, which

may explain why I might have been a little lazy when I wrote my biography of Levi Morton.

Plagiarism (Royal Arsine actually used that word when he telephoned the other day and nagged me yet again about Roger Hopedale) is a malicious term for what may be no more than a borrowed thought or so, or the appropriation of an occasional paragraph when the paragraph in question is superior to one's own. But I know how people, especially those jealous of others' success, view any minor academic sin. That's how my friend Walter Listing explained it during a lunchtime stroll along the Mall, after we'd paid a quick visit to a Caravaggio show at the National Gallery.

"It could be a nasty business, Donald," he said, and squeezed my shoulder firmly.

Although I had known Walter for some time and had come to rely on his wisdom, it was often hard to read his expression, perhaps because his pale face was unlined and, oddly, without noticeable features. I would almost use the word "nondescript" to describe my friend, and perhaps this vagueness, the way he seemed to fade in and out even when he was by my side, made it easier for people to confide in him and advance his career. When we stopped for a hot dog across from one of the museums, I told Walter about my inclination to forever abandon Hobart, and he nodded with apparent approval. "No one ever gave a rat's ass about him," he said, and I have to say that his negative certainty surprised me.

As we strolled about and discussed the upcoming presidential contest (the polls put Gore slightly ahead of Bush), Walter told me that he was thinking of taking up the oboe if Gore won. Then an odd expression—a combination of nostalgia and rage—crossed his face, and I thought how it tormented Walter to think about this statistical closeness, this augury that he might not get the chance to return to his beloved Pentagon. It was also strange to think that when Walter had first worked there, I was a sixth grader in Enola, Pennsylvania. Time flew when I was with Walter Listing, but then none of this—the November election, Roger's manuscript, the Pentagon, our future—seemed important in light of the bad news about Henrietta Hopedale. Sometimes, all of us lose perspective.

WHAT HAPPENED WAS THIS: On a Sunday not long after our lunch in Foggy Bottom, Henrietta invited me to tea, and I naturally thought that I ought to bring along a tape recorder in case she said something worth preserving. "It's too damn hot for tea," she announced when I arrived. I saw that she had set out a pitcher of water and a bag of soggy oatmeal cookies, which I tried my best to ignore.

Henrietta's apartment, close to the Watergate complex on Virginia Avenue, gave one the sense of a far larger life having been compressed into a cramped space. Nothing was very clean or tidy, and an intense, mysterious odor struck me the moment I came through the door. I looked around somewhat desperately for an air conditioner and, finding none, asked if I might open a window.

"They're painted shut," she said, indifferent to my feelings.

Already, as I mopped sweat from my forehead, I regretted having accepted her invitation. As I sipped the chilled water, I was surprised by her appetite—the way she gobbled down seven or eight cookies before I had managed, finally, to chew my way through most of one. Henrietta was in a talkative mood, though, and was soon speaking again about Truman. I was not paying close attention (I had just accidentally bit my tongue) when she lowered her voice and said, "He called it my 'pooshka' every time we made love." At that, I switched on my recorder.

"Your 'pooshka'?"

"That's how he pronounced it," Henrietta said. "Maybe it was something they said in Missouri," which she pronounced "miss-uruh." She kept on this subject for a while longer, and I believe that she might have added more detail—detail I'm quite sure was altogether imaginary—if her son and daughter-in-law hadn't picked that moment to pay an unannounced call.

From the moment Roger and Trudy arrived, I could see that they'd been squabbling and were ready to renew their argument as soon as they could be alone. Roger wore pressed khakis and a blue Lacoste shirt. Trudy had on a polka-dot dress that made her top look larger and softer, though not in a particularly appealing fashion; she looked surprised at seeing me and gave me such a fierce look that I had to turn away. They both seemed weary, in the way one looks when suppressing a grievance, yet for the present they were determined to act as if nothing were the matter.

"What are you guys talking about?" Roger asked, after he'd bent to kiss his mother, and added, with a wink at me, "She hates it when I say 'you guys.'"

"This and that," Henrietta replied.

"It's *that*—I know it's *that!*" Trudy said, a little too loudly, with a glance at me.

"Well of course it's *that,* my dear," Henrietta agreed. "What else would an old lady like me have to offer a handsome young scholar like Donald Frizzé?"

I sensed increasing tension—between Trudy and Henrietta for sure, as well as between Trudy and Roger, but particularly between Trudy and me. I could see that she regarded my tape recorder as if it were an animate object that she'd love to strangle. I tried to think of an excuse to dash off.

"Henrietta, I'm getting concerned," Trudy said in her sweetest voice, and turned to Roger, who seemed even more subdued than usual, although he nodded in agreement.

Seeing Roger made me feel rotten. As far as he knew, I had become a fan of his writing talent, but *Desks of Power* stayed at the bottom of my closet and came to mind only when it rained and I'd notice that a discarded umbrella was sending a small stream of water onto the typescript. I dreaded our unavoidable next lunch at his club, where I still awaited my invitation from the membership committee, and thought that I'd better write down my fibs beforehand. I'm not a very good liar unless I rehearse well.

"I don't see what your concern is, my child," Henrietta said to Trudy.

When Henrietta began saying "my child," an imperious look altered her expression. When she raised her head slightly, as she did while in her "my child" phase, I found myself staring directly into her nostrils, and when her son gave a reciprocal tilt of his head, it was as if four small darkened apertures suddenly, accusingly, were pointed at me.

"It's just that you're embarrassing everyone in our family," Trudy told her mother-in-law. "I've tried not to say this, but I really must." She turned to me and said, "Donald, I know she's telling you her insane Truman fantasy."

Henrietta's expression changed from haughtiness to fury. I could see her jaw tighten and her nostrils appear to widen.

"You deceitful Jew bitch!" Henrietta said.

"Mother, don't," Roger said, gently, walking to her side and resting a hand on her shoulder.

My discomfort was by now intense, and I stared longingly at the window. I was terrified that Henrietta was going to mention Trudy's rumored infidelities, but something else happened: she stiffened, spittle leaked from the side of her mouth, and an instant later she slumped over, as if she were having a seizure. It took all of us a few moments to realize that she actually *was* having a seizure, and a little longer to decide what to do about it. My tape recorder continued to run, but I left it on, ignoring the drain on the AAA batteries, which had cost me several dollars at the CVS on Wisconsin Avenue. Roger knelt at his mother's side. He gripped her hand and asked if she was all right. When she didn't reply, he looked alarmed. "She's not faking," he said.

At this point, I suggested that we call an ambulance or, as an alternative, that one of us take her to a nearby hospital. Trudy said nothing and for just an instant I thought that I detected coldness, or perhaps anticipatory glee, in her eyes, before she said, "Roger, you absolutely must call for outside help." At that point, Roger turned to me and said, "Donald? I can't quite deal with this."

Roger held his mother's hand and stroked her hair. I'm not proud of having been as frozen with indecision as the rest of them, and if Henrietta's chest hadn't risen slowly, I would have guessed that she was dead. But she was definitely breathing, and in the silence the thing that surprised me most was when Trudy said, almost to herself, "We were having a dinner party next weekend, and I suppose now I'll have to cancel it." She shook her head, sadly, and added, "Kissinger was going to be in town and thought he could come." Roger did not seem to hear any of that, and my first thought, which I will blushingly confess, was one of distress that I had not been invited.

Trudy Hopedale

fall, 2000

Eleven

❀

D ONALD FRIZZÉ IS a dear friend, so it's too bad I
can't even begin to tell him about the complications of
my life. I have a feeling he may have heard about Ricardo, but
he's far too discreet to say anything and he knows I would be
distraught if Roger ever found out. It's so sneaky and under-
handed—I know that!—and I feel absolutely awful, and I hope
Donald understands. I also believe that a year from now I'll
still be married to Roger and Ricardo will still be married to
his wife, who hates Washington so much she won't move here.
Perhaps even Donald will be married by then, but I can't imagine to whom.

I've known Donald Frizzé for more than three years, ever since
he called to tell us about some boring forgotten vice president who
once lived in our house. (He said he was going to write a biography of this man, whose name I keep forgetting.) Donald is a mys-

tery to me and to all of my friends. He's so good-looking, but I've never known him to be serious about any woman. He doesn't tell me much about that part of his life, and sometimes I think the only person he's attracted to is himself. It's such a waste, because few single men in this town are as handsome and brilliant as Donald Frizzé. The first time I met him, my knees felt a little weak, and that's a difficult confession for a woman in her forties to make.

One photograph of Donald is my absolute favorite: He's in an armchair, surrounded by books and looking immensely wise. He also seems amused by something he's just heard, and only two or three strands of his shiny dark hair are the least bit out of place—they fall down over his high, distinguished forehead. Even though the photograph is black-and-white, his blue eyes are somehow penetrating. It's easy to see why women fling themselves at Donald; whenever he shows up at the studio, even my associate producer, Marlene DeQuella, looks like she's drooling.

Donald is one of my best guests, not only at my dinner table but on my program. He always has something interesting to say—that's why CBS stole him away—and I only worry that someday he won't have any time left for my little show. But as I say, there are things about Donald I just don't understand, and I've heard some people complain that he's a little too slick and glib. And of course there are whispers that he is gay. People in this town love to whisper.

Roger is one of the people who says that Donald is shallow, and I actually don't think he likes Donald very much, probably because he reminds him of his own shortcomings. Where Roger is tired, Donald is vital, and where Roger pretends to be an artist, Donald is an accomplished historian. I'm fascinated whenever Donald talks about his research, even if I can't always see why he's doing it. I'm so disappointed that our home isn't more historic, but Donald would have told me if it was.

Don't get me wrong. I love Roger dearly, and I'll always be grateful for the life we've made together, even if I can't stand his mother, who always manages to say something mean about me. I was lucky to meet Roger when I did, after he'd already been in those impoverished countries and had just got divorced, and I only wish he enjoyed entertaining. I love it when we can invite people who have something memorable to say, but none of these conversations seem to interest Roger. Still, I know if I hadn't married Roger Hopedale, I might still be Gertrude Weinstein and maybe still living in Detroit. I'm not ashamed of my family; some people love to look down on other people, and that's one thing nobody can accuse me of doing. I'm proud of my late father for selling one of the last DeSoto cars ever made, but it's not something I can talk about with everyone. And my mom is very special. I hate to think how alone she's been since Dad's death, and I wish she would come to visit, but she doesn't like it here. "It's not Washington, it's the people who live there," she explained the last time I invited her to stay with us.

I'm actually getting concerned about Roger. He refuses to let me see that thing he wrote, so of course that makes me a little paranoid. Naturally, I worry that it might have something to do with us—or that people will think it has something to do with us, which is almost as bad. I know he showed it to Donald (I can't imagine why, since he puts Donald down), but Donald won't say anything, even though he usually tells me everything. I wonder what Roger is hiding and why he didn't just write another book about the limits or the paradox or whatever it is of America's power.

MY THING WITH RICARDO was a huge mistake. In the first place, he's not my type. He's too fat and hairy, and he's very pompous, even when we're together, like he's carrying a podium around. But when I had him on my show, I can't deny that something clicked. We flirted; we had fun, especially when he teased me about my reputation as the person who gives the best dinner parties in Washington.

"You've never had me over, not even once," he said, right on the air while we were supposedly discussing some environmental law he opposed.

At first I was so flummoxed that I didn't know what to say, but then I heard myself actually apologize for cancelling our Fourth of July fête—"Everybody's sad about it, but everybody's going to be someplace more important," I explained, feeling as if I'd discarded something very precious—and finally I just blurted, "Well then, Ricardo—Senator Willingham—consider yourself invited to our next little dinner," which is how he ended up at our table that night in May when Donald was there, and Jennifer Pouch (I still remember how they smirked at each other), and that White House aide and his depressed wife, who I hear has left him. I wish I hadn't said all that on the air, because some of my viewers called the station and complained that they felt left out. But on television, I've discovered, what's done is done.

Anyway, after the program, Senator W. invited me to have a drink at a little restaurant in Friendship Heights, and before I knew it, we were in the bar of a hotel and he had ordered two vodka martinis and both of us were gulping them down. It didn't take long before Ricardo said he'd booked a room in that very hotel, and when he said, "Trudy, there's nothing I want more in this world right now than to make love to you," I wasn't all that surprised, although that feeble line sounded awfully scripted. What surprised me was how I reacted.

Ordinarily, I would have found such a declaration deeply offensive, but Ricardo said this in such a sweet, joking way that I just laughed. And I didn't resist when he began to stroke my arm above the elbow, as if he knew I liked that better than just about anything—all the obvious places that men go for. Then, when we were really together for the first time, he seemed so vulnerable, and even a little scared. The truth is, Senator Ricardo Willingham could not quite get it up without some help, which I willingly provided, and as it turned out, the conclusion was quite satisfactory for both of us.

But still: that's where it should have ended, and whenever I come home to my dear Roger, I feel like I've committed a crime. And maybe I have—isn't betrayal horrible? The last thing I want is to hurt my marriage. I can't imagine life without our wonderful home and our friends and our parties, and I hate the distance that seems to be growing between us—oh, I sound like a cheap novel! But I know that when something is set in motion, it eventually has to come to a stop somewhere, and you can't always predict where that will be.

My good friend Jennifer Pouch called from her desk at the *Washington Post* to ask how my mother-in-law was doing, but of course that wasn't her real motive. She started hinting that she knew about Ricardo. It is amazing how fast this sort of story gets around, and of course I pretended I had no idea what she was talking about. I don't believe for a second that Jennifer, who, as I say, is a dear friend, would tell anyone, but people sometimes let things slip, even if those things are hurtful to people they're fond of.

"I know you wouldn't fib to me," Jennifer said, but in a teasing voice, and I said, also teasingly, that I certainly *would* fib if I had to. I can't imagine how Jennifer knew, and all I could think was that someone very malicious and nosy had told her, which is another reason I had better break it off. But I don't want to—that's the problem I'm facing. Despite Ricardo's many, many faults, I enjoy his company; I enjoy the physical side of our relationship, and I would miss it terribly. The only person I could talk to about this is Donald, who would never break a confidence. But I'm almost sure it would ruin something special between us. It's just really worrisome, and it got more so the next time Jennifer brought it up.

"Trudy, Trudy," she said in her second try. "You have to explain why two people have told me you've got something hot going on with the senator. I mean these things just don't come out of nowhere. Did I miss something during that really fun dinner?"

"Jennifer," I replied, "I really don't like being interrogated by good friends. I mean let's say, just to suppose, that I *was* sleeping with a man who was not my husband. Why would I want *any*body to know about it?"

"I think," Jennifer said, "you just told me it's true."

"I certainly did not!" I replied. "I was being very hypothetical."

Poor Jennifer! She's nearly forty, she's never been married, and she's so jealous of other people's happiness. I know she had that one date with Donald Frizzé and that she really likes him, and I know she was very willing to end the evening in one of their beds. But Donald wasn't the least bit interested, and I know how that must have crushed her self-esteem. Jennifer has a nice face, and her body isn't all that bad, but somehow it doesn't go together in a way that attracts men. Also, when she was young—too young, maybe, to know better—she had a really hideous relationship with a cabinet secretary and after he dumped her she wasn't quite the same. I always thought that her aggressive reporting had something to do with that; she's ruined several people in this town, and I sometimes imagine that she has their pictures on her wall, like the heads and antlers of big game. I don't ever want Jennifer Pouch as an enemy, but after our last conversation, when I refused to admit anything, I could sense that she trusted me less than she used to. And I knew that could be bad—maybe even very bad— for me.

Twelve

✿

I REALLY CAN'T STAND most of the people I work with, starting with Marlene DeQuella, my AP, who wants to be an on-air personality like me. Poor Marlene! Then there's Guy Tomanty, who does the weather twice a day and thinks he's just about the funniest man in the world; he can't understand why the networks haven't lined up outside his door to put him on the *Today* show or something. He's so bitter, and everyone can see it when he tries to make us laugh. And then I'm stuck with Pete Plantain, who must be about the worst executive producer in Washington. He's a skinny bald man of about fifty and he has these really bad ideas about how to improve *Trudy's People*. Then, when I tell him it ain't broke, he sulks, just walks away and goes into his office with that pathetic Emmy he won in 1987 and doesn't speak to me for a day or two. Our set is such a cliché—that stupid blue sofa with the Capitol dome behind it—but Pete thinks it's the best thing ever. And he wants me to ask what he calls tough questions—"Be a real journalist, Trudy," he keeps saying—when all he can think of are boring questions that everybody knows the boring answers to anyway. As I keep saying, I want people to be comfortable, like we're all having dinner at my house. If you want the news, tune in at six and eleven and watch some hotshot like Allan Dood, who has a face like a shiny axe.

"But Trudy," Pete said the last time he brought it up, "I don't think people want to be at a dinner party—at least not the party you keep giving."

I try to ignore Pete's insults and his whiny voice, and I keep trying to explain to him that people in this town enjoy being on the inside. Also, I can't force my guests to talk about the Middle East or that horrible attack on an American ship over there or any of that. Even though there's an election and even though, personally, I can't even look at Bill Clinton without thinking about what must have happened and feeling a little sick, I still think people are fascinated by him and by Hillary. "Does he love her?" I said to Pete. "Does she love him? Will their marriage last? Also, how *could* he? That's what we talk about at parties, so why should we do any less for my viewers?"

Pete also thinks that I have Donald Frizzé on too often. I'm tempted to show him the letters we get from viewers, and particularly women who (I know this sounds awful) get moist just thinking about Donald, and I try to tell Pete that we're lucky to book him, what with CBS paying him to be a consultant whenever they need someone to talk about a vice president. I actually can't think of a better guest, and I've told Pete that if Donald can't be on the show, I don't even want to *do* the show. In other words, I'd quit. There are other stations in Washington that would love to have me. The last time I said that, it didn't seem to bother Pete, which I have to admit made me fret a little.

THE OTHER DAY, just before the show, I went into the ladies' room and saw Marlene DeQuella behaving somewhat strangely. She was in front of a sink, staring into a mirror, and reading one of my scripts out loud. She was definitely pretending to be on the air, introducing a guest, and her voice, I have to say, wasn't so bad, although it had a slight Appalachian twang that she'd have to lose. She was shocked when she saw me—she had just said, "And now I'd like you to meet someone who's very special to all of us"—and probably jumped a foot, while the script fell into the basin of the sink. It's lucky she didn't hurt herself.

"I guess you know my secret ambition now," she said. Her face was very red.

"If I were you, Marlene, I'd be just the same," I replied generously, and stood behind her, studying our two faces side by side in the mirror. Her face looked almost apologetic, but she didn't say anything more.

Marlene is pretty in an insipid, blond sort of way. She's maybe twenty-four or twenty-seven and has very light hair, which she probably treats with L'Oréal, and huge boobs, bigger than mine. I've seen Allan Dood looking at her with that lip-smacking expression he has, and I have to say I miss having someone look at me like that. Also she wears tight clothes and on days when they're really tight, it's like she's transfixed Pete Plantain. Later that day, when we were done with the show (thanks to Pete, we had interviewed these two mind-numbing men who worked at the Brookings Institution), Marlene came to the little office I have next to the set and pulled a chair right up to my desk.

"I'm so embarrassed," she said.

"We've all done the same thing from time to time," I assured her.

"I really admire what you do," she said. "I know it must be so hard to ask the right questions and keep everything interesting."

"I've had a lifetime of experience," I replied, exaggerating slightly. I thought for the first time that Marlene might mean well even if she wasn't the highest card in the deck.

"I have such a crush on Donald Frizzé," she said. "He's so hot. I think he's just the best guest you have."

I had suspected that and realized then that Marlene also had a crush on me—nothing sexual, I'm sure, but real enough. Donald, as far as I could tell, had never noticed her.

"I somehow thought you and Allan Dood were an item," I said, continuing what had been our most intimate conversation to date.

"Ugh," Marlene said. "I don't think so."

"And I must say, our friend Pete seems quite taken with you."

At this point, Marlene got up and made sure that the door was closed tight. Then she lowered her voice and said, "Pete has made several—I guess you could call them passes—at me."

"Passes?"

"I mean he hits on me. He makes it pretty clear what he wants."

I shook my head slowly, trying, with every shake, to convey my distress.

"That's intolerable," I said. "He's your boss—someone who can affect your entire career. You should report this. He's twice your age, probably."

"I know, he's more like your age," she whispered. "And the thing is, I *want* him to affect my entire career."

I was having a little trouble following our conversation, but I sensed that Marlene was not quite done with her side of it. She fidgeted and crossed her legs, which I noticed were bare and still tanned. She looked around nervously and then directly at me. I had to admit to myself that some people would consider her beautiful.

"Trudy," she said, and after uttering my name, she fell briefly silent. Then she continued, "I have to just ask you straight out in a real direct way: how would you feel about having a cohost?"

I was so surprised by this question that it was my turn not to speak. Nor did I laugh, although the idea of having two hosts for a program called *Trudy's People* was laughable.

"I'm not sure I understand what you're saying, Marlene," I said, finally.

"This is so embarrassing!"

My opinion of Marlene was shifting rapidly, from indifference to affection to sharp distrust. She seemed, I thought, poised to step on me regardless of my warm feelings.

"There's nothing to be embarrassed about," I said, and tried to smile. "We're all friends here, colleagues trying to work together."

"That's the way Pete put it," she said. "Pete is a little concerned that no one watches the program anymore."

"That's the first I've heard of that," I said, trying to ignore the sudden weight in my stomach. "I know lots of people who watch."

"Oh you know I didn't mean it that way. And I *love* the program. But Pete thinks we could do better, especially with people who are a little younger than middle-aged. And I know he'd hate for you to leave."

There is no point to recounting the rest of our conversation; its direction by then was obvious. My executive producer didn't have the courage to broach any of this to me, so he sent his devious little agent. Well, I said to myself, we would see about that—we would see about a lot of things. But my task at that moment was to keep smiling and, because I'm sometimes not as strong as I want people to think, not to collapse in a puddle of my own tears.

Thirteen

❀

I T ' S   N O T   A S   T H O U G H I've forgotten about Roger's ailing
mother, but it's nearly impossible to keep your mind on only
one thing when you're busy, and of course I did worry about Henrietta—for a while we all thought she wasn't going to make it. But
even though she's eighty-seven, she tries to act my age and that's
probably what keeps her going. I admire that.

I also have to be honest: it hurts that Henrietta has never liked
very much about me and I suppose I've never forgiven her for
saying something I wasn't meant to hear. It was nearly fifteen years
ago, not long after I'd married Roger and we'd just moved into our
wonderful historic home. It was late in the spring, a glorious day
when the tulips were out all red and yellow and the air smelled
clean and we'd had some people over to celebrate our union. I remember standing outside, next to the large French doors that look
over our garden—it's such a wonderful spot, a place where you

can see the tip of the Monument and where planes seem to fly too low on cloudy days—and I believe that I had just finished talking to someone from Vice President Bush's office, who was a close friend at the time. A moment later, I heard Henrietta's voice, which is quite distinctive. She was born in Quincy, and her accent is not Bostonian but very New England, if you know what I mean. She was talking to a snobbish woman who lived on Prospect Place and who, unfortunately, is no longer with us, and I can still recall almost every word.

"I'm very fond of Trudy, really I am, but she is a great puzzle to me," Henrietta was saying. "I'm sure she's very bright and accomplished, but for some reason I don't completely trust her."

"Trudy is young," the other woman said, which was true enough at the time.

"Trudy is what Trudy is always going to be," Henrietta replied. "And I really don't mind that she's Jewish or half-Jewish—her father, the one who sold cars in Detroit. And of course she had all those strange jobs before she landed on television."

It had not taken Henrietta long to discover that I once had to work to pay for college—my father certainly didn't earn much after they stopped making DeSotos. I know she disapproves of what I did to get my degree in art history (my minor was speech), but I'm not ashamed of working in a department store in Ann Arbor or of the few months I spent dancing at a bar in Detroit, where I took off some of my clothes, but not all of them, and definitely never the bottoms. I'm certainly not ashamed of what I did in Washington, working for that senator who got indicted; I was just lucky he remembered me from Ann Arbor, where he had gotten some kind of honorary degree and kept staring at me. Anyway, if I hadn't worked on his committee, I never would have learned how things worked on the Hill and definitely wouldn't have met Roger Hopedale on the day he came to testify about some mean and cruel thing he'd witnessed when he was overseas. Roger looked so distinguished and vigorous then, and his hair was still dark and he was so crazy about me from the moment we met. Of course our backgrounds were different, but I don't think Henrietta could ever understand what it means to work hard to improve yourself. Everything Henrietta ever had was more or less handed to her.

"Look, I don't care, as long as she keeps my son happy," I heard her say. "And Roger seems quite content, no doubt for all sorts of reasons, including the ones we don't like to talk about."

The two women laughed with a naughty squeak, and I blushed slightly, thinking of Roger in his most submissive state. But by then I had heard enough and quietly backed away; I circled around the house to the front door, made my way past the other guests, most of them chatting happily, and managed to greet Henrietta and her friend as if I'd heard nothing. My greeting was effusive, and I planted a friendly peck on Henrietta's wrinkled cheek, leaving a flaming lipstick oval. Despite these efforts, she gave me a suspicious look. My mother-in-law has always been shrewd, and I think she might have guessed that I had overheard—or might even have wanted me to listen. Roger once told me that his father never got along with her, either.

Anyway, Henrietta has been a constant annoyance—always correcting me, always having something to say about my clothes or my friends and, more recently, my television program. Sometimes she berates me for not taking better care of her son, as if Roger is not a grown adult, a person, I'm sorry to say, getting close to old age himself. A few days before she was taken to the hospital, she telephoned and said, "I hate to butt in, my dear child, but I can almost guarantee that Roger feels abandoned these days." Did she know about Ricardo? I had to wonder when she added, "He thinks you care only about yourself and your extracurricular life."

"But Henrietta," I replied, "all I've thought about is myself since the day we got married. You were the first one to point that out."

"Don't be sarcastic, Trudy. You know I'm an old woman and soon you won't have to hear this sort of thing from me."

I hated it when Henrietta talked about her mortality. It's such a cheap way to win sympathy, especially when you're closing in on ninety. Not to be morbid, but we're all going to die someday and that includes Roger and me and Hillary Clinton and everyone else. Even Donald Frizzé will not escape the swoosh of the scythe. But that's okay. Mothers-in-law are entitled, and I know if Roger and I had a child, I would interfere just as much. Sometimes I wish we had, but the whole sperm-and-egg thing didn't work out and we agreed that we weren't going to go crazy trying to improve the odds, although it's not too late for me. Roger is probably relieved, because he has two children of his own from that other marriage, and I've gotten used to the idea of being childless. And by now I've learned to live with Henrietta and her little digs. I just keep quiet when she turns into a mean bitch, and the only thing I haven't gotten used to is her dotty imagination.

I suppose it's possible that she and Thrall knew President Truman way back when, but just a week before she went into the hospital, she nearly ruined a dinner party with her little fantasy. I mean conversation totally halted when she announced that Truman was "the love of my life." Afterward, I told Roger to make her stop.

"It's harmless, Trudy, and I don't see how it hurts to indulge her. It may even be true for all I know. Who can say?"

"*True?*" I replied. "Are you out of your *mind?*"

"Oh, my," Roger said, looking as if it were me who was deranged, patting his hair and tilting his head to turn up his big nostrils. "I don't see who is being harmed by this, my sweet, or why you're getting so exercised."

I couldn't believe my own husband felt this way, and I considered punishing him until I remembered that my behavior with Ricardo was punishment enough. Also, I was starting to suspect that Roger has the same weird Hopedale genes as his mother, at least as far as his writing goes. He keeps reading John Updike and John Grisham—"The two Johns, they're my chief influences," he actually said to me once—and talks a lot about getting to know his fellow Washington writers. But whenever I ask him to show me something, he looks terrified, which makes me wonder. We live in a time when everybody wants to tell everything to everybody, and maybe because of the Clintons, no one seems surprised by anything anymore. People have all sorts of perversions and obsessions and fetishes, and who's to know what interests my husband? I'll even admit that I'm a little unsure about Henrietta: supposing, just supposing it's true, what kind of lover *was* Harry Truman? But I wouldn't say that to anyone. I'd never do anything to puncture the courtesies that keep our little family, and our special city, afloat.

Fourteen

I REALLY DON'T KNOW what to do about Pete Plantain—
whether to complain to corporate, where I know people, or
just tell him he's wrong wrong wrong—but he hasn't had the balls
to even mention that "cohost" idea to me. I kept expecting him to
say something flattering, to plead with me to consider it, but then
he said something so mean-spirited that it took all my self-control
to stay calm and reasonable: he actually came up to me after last
Friday's broadcast and said they might cancel my show at the end
of the year. It was getting "stale," he said, and my guests were
always the same, and blah-blah-blah, all that garbage he's been repeating since Day One. Also, he said, the Clintons would soon be
gone, and then I'd have even less to talk about.

Pete has never understood this town; he doesn't know anyone I
know, and I'm pretty sure he lives in one of those places like
Reston or Gaithersburg that I couldn't find if my life depended on

it. I know that sounds snobbish, which is the last thing a girl from Detroit could ever be, but there is something about those places—people mowing their lawns and going to Home Depot to get things to make their lawns grow faster—that I've tried to get away from for most of my life. I'm sure Pete Plantain would be happy if he could sit all day in his La-Z-Boy and watch the Redskins, which he does starting about now, when it's still too hot and muggy for anyone in his right mind to put on those stupid uniforms. Anyway, I don't know if Pete is serious, or if this is his way of getting me to do what he wants, or if he wants to pay me less when my contract is up, or something else.

Yesterday's program, I'll admit, was a little bit of the same-old same-old: Donald Frizzé was there, talking about Gore and Bush, along with a man who went to St. Albans with Gore but couldn't remember him very well, and a reporter from Dallas, who had this horrible whiny drawl. I had no idea what Donald's point was when he said, "Well, of course Gore is a vice president and Bush is the son of a former vice president, and we've never had an election like that, as far as I can tell," which left everyone just speechless.

I can't imagine who would take over if Pete got rid of me. Marlene DeQuella is too inexperienced (and maybe not quite smart enough, if I'm being brutally honest), and no one would feel comfortable talking to Allan Dood; his teeth are so big, his hair is so greasy. Pete would have to hire somebody from outside, which is never as easy as it looks. He would end up getting someone like me, and if he has to do that, why not me?

Then one day not long ago, Marlene gave me one of those scrunched-up, sad-eyed looks—it was so phony—but of course she couldn't say anything. And Guy Tomanty, our weatherman, walked over and said, "Hey, no one here wants the axe to fall on our dear Trudy, but I keep hearing such terrible things! Say it ain't so." I know Guy is disgruntled about not ever getting to the network, but I gave him a big hug—inside, he's so sweet—and I thought, If I'm going to be canceled, so be it. Everybody gets canceled, even Oprah Winfrey will get canceled one day, I'll bet, and I can't change who I am. Other stations will be thrilled to have me, I'm pretty sure.

I wish Roger was more supportive, but he sounds exactly like Pete when he says the show needs more variety, and he acts like he really doesn't care either way. I know I sound shrill, but Roger lives in another world, and sometimes it's like he believes he's already a big best-selling Washington novelist. I think that's part of what attracted me to Ricardo, who doesn't have many illusions about himself and just likes being a senator. But I feel worse and worse about Ricardo after all these months, and furthermore, he is beginning to repulse me in bed, which seems to be the only thing on his mind. I mean I'm not *that* attractive. The sight of Senator Willingham, who is so identified with trade policy, grunting above me like someone in the middle of a failed push-up, his belly sagging, is so silly that I want to laugh. Sometimes it is okay with him—I'll admit it's been a lot better than okay—but I wish it wasn't such a strain for Ricardo, who still has trouble getting his thing up and then shivers and does that "Trudy, sweet Trudy!" routine. Oh, well, it has to end soon, and then I'll be glad that we never got caught, even though more people are a little suspicious and Jennifer Pouch is dying to tell someone what she thinks she knows. I ought to invite Jennifer on my show more often, even though she's not very good on camera because she blinks too much and the audience seems to hate her, to judge from the letters. She may be a little younger than me, but she looks a lot older. She looks older every week.

AT THE BEGINNING of October, I told Roger that I wanted to have a major dinner party, and then we had a squabble when he insisted that we had to ask his mother, who was just home from the hospital and feeling much better.

"I love Henrietta too," I said. "As you know. But we don't want to overtire her."

"She can leave early if she feels tired," Roger said. "I'll just call a cab."

"Also," I continued, "she does seem out of control, don't you think?"

"I think you're being intolerant," Roger said, in that huffy way he has when he runs out of logical arguments.

"I'm truly trying to do what's best for her," I said, hoping to make Roger understand. "If she keeps saying some of the things she's been saying, people will laugh at her. I hate seeing that. She's so vulnerable."

"People wouldn't dare laugh," Roger replied.

This was very delicate, because I didn't want Roger to become angry and I didn't want to insult his mother, either. So I changed the subject or, perhaps more accurately, moved the subject to another interior shelf.

"Let's have twenty-four people and three tables," I said, and pretended not to notice Roger's look of terrible pain. He hated these productions, as he called them. And he hated the idea of me as a "Washington hostess," which is the last thing I am. Also, as I've told Roger numerous times, I can't see the point of living in an amazing town like ours and not being in the absolute center of the action, particularly if you *can* be there. That's Donald Frizzé's theory, and no one is more in the midst of things than Donald, who went to dinner and a movie at the White House be-cause—and I say this as a friend—he's such a suck-up. Lastly— and I didn't tell Roger this—a major party might be a way to get Pete Plantain back onto the reservation; we could always seat him next to someone we had to invite, like Henrietta. I guess, now that I think about it (and I have thought about it a lot), I really don't want to lose my show. But I'll never let on how I feel not to Pete, not to Donald, not even to Roger, even though there are times, I have to say, when keeping it all inside me makes me feel horribly alone.

Fifteen

❧

I SUPPOSE SOME PEOPLE would say I overstepped, but I have to look at it in a practical way: if Roger doesn't find out, it won't matter; and he won't find out, so what's the harm? I know that sounds dishonest, but I had been so worried about him.

Roger's study is sort of off-limits, and I respect that. Even our cleaning lady has to stay away—she probably thinks he collects pornography or something. But of course one reason Roger likes to keep it private is because the shelves are not only filled with books by his "influences" but with mementoes of his life prior to me. He must know it wouldn't exactly thrill me to see pictures of his first wife, Louise, who everyone says is so nice, and their two children, who are grown and who we never see, which certainly isn't my fault. (His son is a lawyer in Boston and his daughter does fund-raising for various charities in Richmond, where her husband is some sort of developer.) Roger never explained why they got divorced, but I think it had something to do with Louise falling in love with someone else.

I know that Roger is in touch with his children and sees them when they're in town, but I don't think he ever speaks to Louise, whose next husband died a year or so after they got married. It just goes to show that you can't count on anything. But I try not to think about that because it makes me sad. I hate to think how we all get old. My mom is way over seventy now, and whenever we talk I feel extra sad because I know she wishes I'd married someone like Barry, my college boyfriend, who wanted me to stay in Detroit. Of course getting old isn't the worst thing. At least I know what I mean to people in this town, no matter how many wrinkles I get. For someone like Marlene DeQuella, though, in twenty years—well, thirty years—it will be completely different. I don't feel competitive with Marlene, who doesn't have very much talent, but I also don't appreciate the way they're forcing her on me.

Anyway, I really do think a wife is entitled to know if her husband is hiding something, and the same goes for husbands. Roger knows everything about me, except for what would hurt him. Thank goodness, Ricardo is just about over. The last time we did it, he totally collapsed on top of me. I was afraid he had died or something and all I could think was how to explain *that* one away. He was still snoring when I pushed him off and got dressed, and he hasn't called me since.

Anyway, I didn't feel quite right going into Roger's study and poking around his desk drawers until I found his sacred manuscript. I promised myself I'd just read a few pages. That way I'd get the idea, which I needed to have if I was to share in Roger's life and understand him better, and also to give him advice. So I did it, and now I only wish I hadn't because some things you simply can't forget. One chapter of that wretched book was enough—one *page* would have been enough!—and the whole time I kept thinking, one, that this was written by a man I thought I knew, and, two, how desperately I wanted to keep *Desks of Power* away from everyone in the world—for Roger's sake more than mine. I even thought of burning it, just like Hedda Gabler did to that poor suicidal man, but of course Hedda didn't love her husband the way I love Roger and she wouldn't have known what to do with a modern-day computer, blinking like it knows what you're thinking. I might have burned the computer if I could have done that without finishing off our beautiful home. Anyway, this much of it was more than enough for me:

> . . . Mitch MacPeters knew that finding the remains of The Interrogator in his closet was not mere happenstance. The last time he had seen him alive, The Interrogator and Tony Snike had just completed their mission, something so bloodstained that, if revealed, could bring shame to the nation and might also cost Snike crucial votes at confirmation. The Interrogator looked older than he used to look when he was alive but, in a curious way, better. MacPeters, as he stared, understood how easily he might come under suspicion.

When he heard Tammy Roberts's sharp rap on his outer door, he hurriedly closed the closet. In the few minutes that his AA had been away, she had done something to herself. Her breasts looked bolder, her hips wider, and her pink, plush parted lips fuller. He had an overpowering urge to grasp her, as if to protect her from something evil he felt hovering close by. Her mouth, like a soft orchid, was trembling.

"I just got a call," she whispered. "From a man who told me to look inside your closet."

"My closet?"

"That one," she said, pointing. "His voice scared me."

MacPeters nodded. Now he had to decide whether to tell his trusted aide what he had found minutes earlier. The body, he believed, would raise fresh questions.

"Tammy," he said, making every effort to appear calm, "you were right to be alarmed."

As his AA's eyes asked the unspoken question, MacPeters gently gripped her elbow; the knob on the closet door glimmered faintly, like a golden mushroom.

"See for yourself," he said, and fought off an odd, nervous impulse to chuckle.

She covered her moist mouth as if suppressing a scream. They could see that rigor mortis had begun to take effect, and that the face of the dead man had a tight silvery sheen of agony.

"I've never met him," she said.

"I knew him long ago, just casually," MacPeters replied,

wondering if he should tell Tammy something more about the diplomatic errands he undertook in Central America long before he ran for office—a succession of triumphs that led him from the courthouse as district attorney to the statehouse as an assemblyman and now this, the big house, the pinnacle. Perhaps he, too, had made mistakes, but he regretted them—more than he could say for Tony Snike. MacPeters recalled Snike in his camouflage getup, his beetle-sized mustache moist with sweat, the sight of fresh, thick blood on his curved thumb. He knew with exactitudinous certainty what Tammy was thinking.

"You believe I did this, don't you?"

She shook her head, with her lips shaking and her pink rippled tongue briefly visible.

"I can't believe that, Senator—I won't. But security is so tight in the building, it would be hard for anyone else to haul a body around and, you know . . ." Her voice trailed off.

"I know what you're saying." He sighed. "But I swear to you, I know nothing about this."

The desktop telephone rang again. This time, before MacPeters lifted the receiver, he beckoned Tammy to his side, inviting her to put an ear, that pearly pinkish oval, next to his. He inhaled her perfume and tried not to notice her radiant warmth, the supple pressures, the outlines of her nipples like mysterious acorns, the sweet, dark furrows of her neck, and he would not allow himself to dwell on what surely lay just above the smooth convexities of her polished round knees. His eyes went from the window, which framed the stiff, pointed Monument, and then, as the caller spoke, to his loyal womanly aide.

"I hope you found your little surprise, MacPeters," the voice said.

"*Senator* MacPeters."

The caller chuckled and hung up with a soft click.

MacPeters returned the phone to its cradle, but Tammy remained, her cheek touching his, her hip gently brushing him. When she turned, she was pressed against the senator's throbbing prick, and he said, "I don't know what they want, but I have to admit that it worries me." Then, in a quiet voice, he added, "Back then, when we were young and inexperienced, we never thought enough about the limits of our power, the edge of our might, of America's image in the world, or, paradoxically, what our leaders . . ."

Oh my God, oh my God, so who can I talk to about this? Not Jennifer Pouch, who will listen oh, so sympathetically and then blabber to everyone we know. Sometimes I think Jennifer thrives on other people's woes. Just the other day, we had a "ladies' lunch" at Barclay's, a place I hate but journalist types like because they get to see each other, even though they see each other all the time and talk about themselves—and also I'm so tired of Walter Johnson's old uniform in the glass case and all that memorabilia that tourists go to see. Jennifer has never learned how to dress, and it's like everything she wears comes from Hecht's. Also, I have no idea where she gets her hair done, and I would advise her to see Jean-Didier at Raquel's, except it would sound wrong if I said that—like a personal criticism. Her hair is kind of limp and has those weird streaks, like a striped cat, and maybe she should get it cut short, though it's not for me to say.

Jennifer could actually be quite attractive if she took a little time with herself and lost some weight, maybe fifteen pounds, maybe twenty, although there would still be that thing about her that men don't like. Every time I see her, I realize she's totally given up on the meaningful part of life and has settled for casual sex and a career. I feel very, very sorry for Jennifer. But she is usually fun because she's always full of good information and is never stingy about passing on everything she knows. That's one of the reasons she's such a good guest, and it's why she's a little scary, like when she seems to know more than you do. She's more than scary when you realize that she's trying to get something out of you, and at our lunch I got that idea almost from the first bite, like when Jennifer gave me that crooked, conspiratorial smile and said, "So tell me, Trudy, what's happening over at your television station. I hear these rumors."

I tried to think of a reply, and of course I knew that she'd been saving up that question from the moment we'd made our lunch date. "I hear all sorts of stories," she added, "and they make me worry about how they're treating you."

I tried to smile back at Jennifer. Then I attempted a bite of my lobster salad, which repelled me with its gooey pink surface. When I dipped into it, my fork shook, and I dropped some of it on my lap—mayonnaise and all; and Jennifer, being a good reporter, noticed everything and said nothing. If Jennifer ever got a look at what Roger had written, I don't think I could stand it.

Sixteen

S OMETIMES I THINK I don't know anyone very well, starting, maybe, with myself. The other day—probably because it's
almost Halloween—I thought about when I was little and how I
put on costumes and pretended to be anything, including a pilot
and a movie star and a reporter like Dorothy Kilgallen. I guess I
still pretend, like when I look in a mirror and try out different ex-
pressions and ways to nod my head and imagine I'm Barbara Wal-
ters. I suppose that makes me seem self-absorbed, but I think it
helps me when I commune with my reflection, and the other day I
promised to be a better person—I mean I started talking out loud
like a crazy lady. "Well, Trudy Hopedale, aren't you proud?" I said
to myself. "You're acting like everything is just swell, but you could
lose your television program, you've spied on your husband, and
you've let a man you hardly know stick his penis in you." I stared
into my hazel eyes, feeling really ashamed, and vowed never again

to have Senator Willingham on my show and definitely not to invite him to dinner at our house.

Speaking of which, it's almost settled that my program is going to be called *Lunch with Trudy & Marlene,* and I have to admit it doesn't sound all that bad. Also, my name comes first, so everyone will know it's still my show and that Marlene is like my helper. But I'm not fooling myself, either. It won't be the same, and it's not that much fun to come to work anymore. I can't stand the way people stare, almost as if they're feeling some kind of pity. When Allan Dood looks at me, I feel like some scrap he would feed a dog. His teeth really are huge.

I really don't know who to talk to about the way I'm feeling— definitely not Jennifer Pouch and probably not Donald Frizzé, either, and when I call my mom, she just sounds like a mom and a schoolteacher and tells me everything will work out in the end. As for Donald, I'm finally starting to realize how secretive he is. For instance, I know he has this close friend, an older-type man named Walter Listing, who used to work in the Pentagon and shows up at lots of parties around town. But Donald has never once introduced us; it's like he's ashamed. He refuses to talk about Jennifer Pouch, not one word, and no matter how many hints I drop, he won't say if he takes my mother-in-law's delusions the least bit seriously. The last time I called, there was something in his voice that he held back, even when he said, "Hi, Trudy."

"You've been a stranger," I said, even though only two or three days had elapsed since our last conversation.

"I can't tell you how busy I've been. I'm absolutely desperate to find another subject for my next book."

Donald is so bad. This is the first time he's said that he's finally dropping that biography about the man whose name I can never remember.

"You haven't asked about Henrietta," I said.

"Still on the mend, I presume?"

"That's not what I meant."

Donald's silence was answer enough, and I got so annoyed that I came close to hanging up. Instead, I opened another avenue of inquiry. There are times when my techniques as an interviewer, while not as polished as Jennifer's, come in handy.

"I'm aware," I said, "that you've read Roger's first stab at fiction. Would you please tell me—and I'm talking to you as a friend—if you think he's done something worthwhile."

There followed another of those little pauses that were beginning to irritate me.

"Trudy," he said, finally, "this really has to be something between myself and Roger. It has nothing to do with our friendship."

"I understand," I said. "But I'd love to have some hint—a glimmer, a clue of a clue—as to whether you consider this project worthwhile or an embarrassment to me and the entire Hopedale family. I think I'm entitled to ask that."

"Again, Trudy, you're asking me—"

I interrupted him because his insipid little replies were taking me past irritation and into full annoyance.

"Oh, Donald," I said, "if you thought Roger's little novel had the tiniest bit of merit, I really believe you'd say so. You wouldn't hem and haw and dither like an old woman. So I'm taking this as a sign you think it's shit. Is that fair?"

"You're trying to trick me," he said, his voice slightly altered, "and I'm not going to let myself be tricked."

"You're saying it's shit," I declared, and when he said nothing to refute that, I added, "I give up," and at least had the satisfaction of slamming down the receiver. I hoped he got an earful, but it didn't make me all that happy to have done it.

I HATE SQUABBLING with friends, and Donald has been such a good and loyal friend that I couldn't stay mad at him. When he came on the show again in November, a week after our very weird national election (Donald says we might not know the winner for years and like everyone else on television he couldn't stop talking about Tilden and Hayes), I really hoped that things were all patched up between us. But I also should have known I couldn't trust Marlene DeQuella, my new junior partner or, as she calls herself, "cohost."

Marlene flirted with Donald in a way that made me ashamed for her. As soon as he arrived, she breathed into his face and pressed her bosoms against him and pulled on his sleeve. Donald looked uncomfortable, which made me happy; it's so pathetic the way men fall apart when a woman gets close and sends those signals, and Marlene was laying it on about as thick as anyone could. "Oh, Donald, you're just our best guest, you give everything such amazing perspective." She gushed so much that he could hardly manage a reply. I can't believe I ever thought it would work out with me and Marlene. What's really unbelievable is that Pete Plantain thinks she's wonderful and keeps saying so, which I find very demoralizing. Whenever he even sees her, a little vein in his bald head begins to throb.

But none of that is nearly as important to me as making things right at home. It's just a feeling I have, but it's like Roger hasn't been himself. Maybe he's heard talk about me, although I think I would have known if anyone had told him about the senator, which I feel so ashamed about now, or maybe he's guessed that I've looked around in his little study. All I know is that it hasn't been the same for a while. When we're in bed, he turns over and barely manages a cordial good night. I know he doesn't like to do it as much as he used to, but still: when we first got married, even though he wasn't a kid, he'd attack me every night and sometimes twice if he got all worked up, and he loved to wake me up in the morning and do it again with me on top. Now it's been at least three weeks, and even then, it wasn't much. I hardly noticed he was there, if you know what I mean.

I'm the first to admit that it's probably my fault. We don't talk much anymore about serious things, not even about the recount in Florida, which I find pretty exciting and gives us something to discuss every day on my show, and I know Roger's a little resentful because he doesn't have all that much to do and I've been so successful. I think he expected to hear something—even if it was just an encouraging word—from somebody close to "Dubya," because Roger was so devoted to the first Mr. Bush.

Also, I know he doesn't appreciate my comments about his mother. I don't want to be snide, and I don't think I'm a naturally snide person, but Henrietta *is* turning into even more of a spiteful old bitch and there's something not quite right in her head when she has those demented imaginings. Like mother like son, I'm starting to think, after reading that smidgen of Roger's novel, and then, I have to admit, going back to his study once more to see if there were other parts that might offend me or our friends. I did find a few things (sex things) that were really disturbing—they didn't sound at all like Roger—and a lot of words that he'd never say out loud. After that, I didn't need to read more, not unless I wanted to see how it ended, which I didn't. It just made me more upset—or maybe sad. It was as if Roger was getting more satisfaction from his imaginary woman—that Tammy character with her buttons open—than from the real me. What if someone actually liked his sick imagination and wanted to publish it? I could see how the life we'd so carefully built together could crumble, and how I could become a laughingstock and then be forgotten, in that order.

Seventeen

❧

I HAD HEARD ABOUT Royal Arsine because Roger had mentioned him now and then over the years, although never in a nice way—I think it was something about working "beyond the parameters" and being expelled from some poor country for abusing tribesmen. And of course I'd read about him very recently because if the young Bush ever wins this nerve-wracking election, Arsine may get some big government job. But I'd never met him, and so when he called me at home and asked me to meet him for breakfast, it was a total surprise. I said okay, mostly out of curiosity, even though breakfast is not my best time of day.

Royal Arsine is one of those people you think of as being memorable, and not only for the way they look but because of the way they look *at* you. He has genuinely beady eyes (I mean they look like beads), a mustache shaped like a water bug, and he appears almost young until you get close and see the wrinkles and the gray hair and those little eyes, like a frog's. Or at least that was my impression—and it was enough to almost make me turn right around and walk away from the restaurant. He was sitting in a corner booth reading the newspaper and shaking his head, probably because every story was about counting votes in Florida, which was starting to drive everyone in town absolutely crazy and must be a lot worse for someone who has a big stake in it. He would have been so easy to spot even if he wasn't the only one there, especially when he looked at me with his BB eyes like I'd committed some sort of criminal deed. It was all a little mystifying, but I guessed that he liked to do that to people; maybe it gave his life more meaning. That's probably why he wanted me to come to the Rouge Canine, a place where something happened during some crisis in the sixties. Everything was a crisis back then.

"I'm grateful you found the time on such short notice," he said, with a sort of overdone politeness that might have been sarcasm. Arsine had a great voice, very sonorous, with one of those sophisticated accents that you hear in old movies, a little like William Powell. He wore a white shirt, a blue blazer, and a dark green tie. His hair was shiny and his part was just over his right ear. But I couldn't look at him because his eyes—I know I can't stop talking about them—were like two stones, and they didn't seem to be focused on me, or anything.

"Mr. Arsine—"

"Call me Roy," he said. Even though he faced me, he seemed to be looking elsewhere.

"Roy," I said. "I have to tell you I'm extremely curious. It has to be something about Roger's career, doesn't it?" I was pleased with my businesslike tone.

"Your husband and I go back a ways," he said, as if I hadn't known that they were acquainted.

"A lot of Roger goes back a ways," I replied, and smiled so that he would know I was trying to be amusing.

There was something really odd about his expression then, as if I were an object that merited closer study.

"Of course you've only known Roger in a certain way," he said. "During a certain period."

"I'm sorry, Mr. Arsine—"

"Roy," he insisted.

"Yes, Roy, but you're speaking to me as if you're conducting some sort of investigation."

My reply made him stop, or at least brought a moment of strained silence.

"May I call you Trudy?" he asked, and before I could reply, he said, "Trudy, think of this as a conversation—nothing more."

"That's fine," I replied, "but what is it that you actually want, Mr. Arsine?"

It was about then that a waiter intervened, plunking down plastic-coated menus that had large dimensions but a limited number of choices. Because it was not yet eight-thirty in the morning and I was not quite myself, the decor made me a little dizzy. The inside was reddish—the booths had bright red leather seats—and when I looked around, it was like everything was on fire. I asked for a scone and a cup of tea and Royal Arsine said that he was content with his coffee, which looked cold to me. I had the feeling that the waiter, a Latino whose long hair was in a ponytail, was anxious to please him.

"Mr. Arsine," I began.

"Roy," he said with, I sensed, some impatience.

"Roy," I continued, "I have no idea what you want, or in what capacity you want it. And I have to tell you that you're starting to make me nervous."

"Fair enough," he said. "But like I said, Trudy, this is just a conversation."

"I get the idea, but what I still don't get is what you want to converse about."

Then he sort of leaned back in his chair and moved his head, still not quite looking at me, and said, "It's more what I *don't* want, Trudy. I *don't* want to be embarrassed by your husband."

This was getting very weird, and all I could say was "Why would he do that? Roger Hopedale has served his country as a diplomat, and he is very wise, as his book on the paradoxical limits of American power will tell you. How could that possibly embarrass you?"

He shook his head and took a sip of his chilly coffee.

"You're aware that he's written another sort of book?" he asked.

I nodded, although I didn't like the way he phrased that assertion, and now I could see where the conversation was heading.

"And you're aware," he went on, "that Roger and I once worked together as partners, during one of his stints abroad?"

"To tell you the truth," I said, "I'm not aware of any 'stint,' as you put it, or any partnership with you, although he certainly knew *about* you. Were you with the embassy too?"

As he put down his coffee, he somehow managed to simultaneously withdraw from his jacket a short ballpoint pen and a small notebook, in which he jotted something with great swiftness. I was about to ask what had become so interesting when he stopped writing and fixed his tiny eyes on mine.

"Perhaps it's nothing," he said, more to himself than to me.

Then he reached across the table and patted the back of my hand with his fingertips, which—and maybe I'm exaggerating—felt icy. I suppose that he tried to smile, but his mouth went into a bizarre angle, and I realized that it was a fault line in his face. I wasn't the least bit hungry, but now I was committed to my scone, which had just arrived. I tried to think of something that would make me sound clever and finally said, "You're baffling me," with one of my most appealing smiles. "Now tell me the real reason we're having this morning snack."

Because he didn't answer me right away, I set upon the scone, pretending not to notice when it broke apart and hundreds of crumbs tumbled onto my plate.

"They're always a little stale here," he said. Then he just looked at me for what seemed like a long time and finally said, "Look, Trudy, long story short, I need you to let me see the novel or whatever it is he's working on. I have to be sure he's not giving away secrets to those who wish us harm."

"You're confusing me," I said.

Arsine shook his head and said, "Think of it as an insurance policy for your hubby. He'll never know."

I shook my head. "I can't help you—it would feel very wrong," I said, and at that he smiled in a nasty way.

"He showed it to your friend," he said, "the fellow who calls himself Donald Frizzé."

There he was again, trying to be mysterious, and not doing it all that well.

I know that I raised my voice a little then. "Donald Frizzé," I informed him, "is a distinguished vice presidential historian. I don't know you very well, Mr. Arsine—"

"Roy—"

"Roy, but you have a way of making everything sound very low and mean and you treat me like I'm naïve. Also, I suppose Donald wouldn't show it to you either, which is very honorable of him." As I said that, I felt proud of Donald.

Then, as if he'd been storing it up, Royal Arsine started to demean my friend. I didn't want to listen, but I couldn't help hearing his vicious little recitation—that Donald was a joke to his peers. When this horrid man used the word "plagiarism," I just got up, unwilling to hear another word. And then I walked out without even saying good-bye. He didn't say good-bye, either.

Outside, the air was chilly, but it felt refreshing and the Christmas decorations along Wisconsin Avenue made me think of the parties ahead and the season and of course the arrival of a new administration, whoever was going to be in charge. People were going to work (horns were beeping) and I watched some of them as they sat in their cars, chatting on their cell phones and listening to their radios, barely moving. I didn't recognize anyone. Only later did it occur to me that Royal Arsine was not only trying to punish poor Donald Frizzé but would be more than willing to punish me as well.

Eighteen

❦

S TARTING AROUND THANKSGIVING, I always think about what I can only call my blessings: my friends, my career, my good fortune to be living in a place that's so vital to the entire world. It is extra exciting when a new administration moves in, and naturally it's a huge relief to finally have this insane election settled so everyone can just change the subject. It was getting so boring—the broken ballots, those sickly smiles from all the wrinkly lawyers in their dark suits. I have to admit I wish Al Gore had won because we all know him, but Roger points out that everyone knows the old George Bush too and they keep saying that his son is much smarter than he sounds.

I just wish Roger wouldn't get his hopes up; the phone still hasn't rung with any kind of encouraging offer and I seriously doubt that it will. I mean everyone wants these new appointments, and wherever I go, even to get my hair done at Raquel's, I hear about someone moving to town. My friend Gail Tachyon, who sold us our house right after Roger and I got married (I still wish we hadn't paid the ridiculous asking price), told me that her phone never stops ringing, even though she never sells in Virginia, where lots of the new people want to live.

It's certainly going to feel different after the last eight years, even if most of the newcomers aren't all that new and they've been living here all along, like in hiding. But while it's good to see auld acquaintance, it does make it harder to talk about something fresh. I think that's one of the problems we're having with *Lunch with Trudy & Marlene*. But what are we supposed to talk about? I wish someone would tell me instead of criticizing all the time.

What's hardest to get used to is the way people pay more attention to my so-called cohost than they do to me. It's like whenever I go past Pete Plantain's office, I see her in there. She's always wearing partly buttoned blouses and those short skirts that go way up past everything, and when that little vein in Pete's head begins to throb, it's not hard to figure out where his eyeballs are. Sometimes he looks almost cross-eyed when they're together and he doesn't seem to hear what I'm saying. I've always heard that when women reach a certain age, they become invisible to men, but I never imagined it would happen to me and I truthfully can't believe it has. Royal Arsine sure seemed interested when we had that breakfast, the way he touched my hand with his fingers (ugh!), and I'm not even going to mention Senator Willingham, who more than once looked like he was going to die in all the excitement, the way his eyeballs rolled up when he had his little twitchy climax and began to lick my ears. I'm still so ashamed.

But I'm realistic enough to know I can't compete with someone like Marlene DeQuella, not when she comes to the table with those pendulous boobs and that vacant look that makes men want to crawl on their knees and beg. That's how Pete acts, and that's why I believe Pete is going to get rid of me as soon as he decently can. I'm getting those pitying looks again from Marlene and from Guy Tomanty, our miserable weatherman, and from everybody else.

Anyway, my concerns seem a little trivial when you think about what's really important. I'm not only referring to our election but to the Middle East and starving people in Africa and all over the world and permanent things like death and disfigurement. I'm thinking in that somber vein because it's struck home in a real way: two weeks before Christmas, Roger's mother went back into the hospital, and this time it looks like she isn't coming out. That's what Roger thinks, anyway. When he came back from the emergency room, he said, "This is it, Trudy," in an angry, accusing tone that I'm not sure I understood, and he seemed so depressed that I didn't even offer him a sip of my gin and tonic. I know that he blames me for the fit, or whatever medical term they use to describe what Henrietta had. Nothing could be more unfair.

All I know is that we'd been having a relaxed Sunday dinner at home, with just Roger and his mother, along with Donald Frizzé. I know: I should never have invited Donald, who made me furious the way he kept egging on Henrietta—prying actually, despite my protestations. But he is such a special friend, almost like family, and I know he's often alone on Sunday evenings. Also, I've started to worry about Donald after what Royal Arsine insinuated about him, and I would hate to see him hurt by something he may have done long ago. Anyway, I kept hoping that Donald would stop asking Henrietta those annoying questions, especially when I kicked him under the table, and pretty hard at that. But he didn't stop, and neither did Henrietta, even when I pleaded and said that her reveries—I wish now I'd chosen another word—were totally inappropriate for a woman who was about to have her eighty-eighth birthday.

"My beloved Trudy," she replied in what I'm sure she thought sounded like a reasonable voice, "I hope you're not suggesting that I'm some batty old dame who's making this up."

When I refused to take her bait, Roger looked at me sternly and Donald brushed back his lustrous hair and looked away. But if one cannot speak frankly in the presence of one's family, what is the point of speaking at all? We had by that point finished the chicken course and perhaps we'd all had a bit too much wine, although I'm sure I was absolutely sober. But basically the mood was cheerful and familial and I'd even set out little petits fours and candles surrounded by greenery to put a happy accent on the good preholiday spirits in our dining room. The truth is, I felt kindly toward the matriarch of the Hopedale family and thought for a moment or so that I might miss her when she was no longer with us. But even as I had that generous impulse, it never occurred to me that such a time would arrive so speedily.

"Oh, Henrietta," I said after she repeated more of her silly nonsense, "you know we all love you, and I can't imagine a better mother-in-law. But we all know how our memories play tricks. There are times when I can't remember if I saw a certain movie with Roger or with someone else. Sometimes I have to work out the date and go from there."

At the sound of his name, Roger turned to me again, and his eyes, as he blinked, appeared to flash semaphorically. Donald, who had just asked yet another unacceptable question ("Where did the Secret Service go when you were intimate?"), leaned forward, his hair tumbling over his handsome forehead, his beautiful bluish eyes intense. Henrietta, though, did not appear to hear Donald, and turned to me.

"I know what you're implying, Trudy," she said, "and I don't like it. Not one bit. It's that Jewish suspicion you have."

"I'm not implying anything," I said, smiling as pleasantly as I could at a woman I respected deeply and, despite our minor differences, loved. "Also," I added, still smiling, "my father was the least suspicious person who ever lived."

"You're telling me that I can't remember the difference between Harry Truman and some schoolboy who fondled me," Henrietta said. "What if I said you couldn't remember who groped you in the backseat of—what did your poor father sell? De*Sotos*?"

"Henrietta, please don't take offense," I said.

"Nothing like this ever happened to you—not where you come from," she said, and although I might have become angry, I acted as if nothing she said was wounding. I tried to remember that she was a very old woman and also my husband's mother when I said, "Of course you're right—I don't know what got into me." But even those words did not mollify her.

"First you accuse me of lying and then you patronize me," she replied, and her face became increasingly dark as, in a cascade of unfairness, she spoke these words. A few seconds later, while Roger was saying, "Mother, please," and Donald was saying, "Henrietta, I don't think that is what Trudy intended," she fell off her chair, a soft landing that certainly didn't break any of her fragile bones but did leave her immobilized, lying on her back with her four limbs curiously raised (I thought momentarily of paws). That is the image of Henrietta Hopedale that I am afraid will always haunt me, not least because it is a reminder of our universal fragility, those shadows that come to all of us in the hours before dawn when we might imagine ourselves—and everyone—on our backs, our limbs raised. As for Henrietta, I quite naturally worried that people would hear about this horrifying episode and, as Roger so unjustly did, put a tiny portion of the blame on me.

Nineteen

H ENRIETTA'S DECLINE was so fast that I never managed to see her again. I did keep meaning to stop by the hospital and I believe that she was aware of my intentions, but we all get so busy and preoccupied (those of us outside hospitals), and between my program and the holidays and everything, the time just got away. Perhaps it's just as well, because I'm not certain that she would have enjoyed my company, although deep down I believe she was just as fond of me as I was of her. In any case, the point is somewhat moot, and furthermore Roger was always by her side, which was the important thing. I give him credit for being a devoted son and wonder if he'd be even half as sweet with me.

Anyway, Henrietta passed away on Christmas Eve, which is not the most convenient time of the year to do that, although I'm not complaining. But it did throw something of a monkey wrench into our holiday plans. Because *Lunch with Trudy & Marlene* was on hiatus between Christmas and New Year's, Roger and I had planned to take a few days in a warm, relaxing place like Saint Bart's or Belize. I know that may sound a little selfish and maybe I don't seem particularly sad, but when you're old and have had such a full life, there's not all that much to be sad about if you ask me. Of course Roger will miss her, just like I still miss my dad, who was a lot younger when he died. And naturally I'll miss Henrietta too.

This has been a hideous time—there's no getting away from that. While the rest of Washington is having all those pre-Inaugural parties and getting ready to welcome a brand-new president (we've been invited to several receptions, although not yet to the swearing-in), we have to plan a funeral. At least we have the grave site picked out, next to Thrall Hopedale, and, luckily, that beautiful Georgetown church where Roger likes to worship is available. But the hard part is still to come: we have to decide who to invite to the reception, or whatever you call it, after the service, and I suppose I have to hire a caterer. I've tried to get Roger to focus on these details, but whenever I nudge him to be practical, he becomes disagreeable.

"Trudy," he actually said, "you keep talking about my mother's funeral as if you were giving one of your dinner parties. I wonder if you have any idea how this has affected me."

Roger always looked tired in the morning (maybe I do too), but lately there's been an old man's crankiness in his manner that I can't get used to—as if he had decided to jettison simple courtesy. I know he was grieving, just like me, but I have to wonder if he's harboring some smoldering grudge. This wasn't going to be easy for me, either, especially when I have to deal with Roger's first wife and his adult children, and there was always the risk that someone might want to stay overnight in an extra bedroom, which would leave us no breathing room at all. Then there was the Donald Frizzé problem, or whatever one calls it when a good friend turns into an interminable nag.

"I was so sorry to hear about your loss," Donald said when he called, speaking in his most oozing voice.

"Thank you, sweetie," I replied. "It's more Roger's loss than mine, but it is a difficult time for all of us."

"I'll send a note to Roger," he said.

"An e-mail will do."

I knew very well what Donald wanted, but I wasn't going to help, not even when I heard him clearing his throat and searching, no doubt, for just the right way to phrase his little request.

"I wonder what's going to happen to her things," he said after I'd waited him out.

"Her *things*?" I replied. "Are you worried about her clothes and knickknacks and *medicine* bottles?" I paused, and when the silence went on long enough, I said, "Never mind, Donald, I know very well what you're after."

"I'm aware this isn't your favorite subject, Trudy."

"It certainly is not."

"And of course I'm almost certain we're talking about a person whose grip on reality had slipped a bit."

Donald wasn't fooling me, and I wasn't going to let him get away with thinking that he was.

"You're dying to find something incriminating, aren't you?" I asked. "Admit it, Donald."

"I'm a historian," he replied. "I don't want to intrude upon this period of family sadness, but I can never stop being what I am."

"Don't patronize me," I said, sounding, I realized, a little like my late mother-in-law.

I can't completely explain why I was being so mean. Maybe because I felt the whole world was being mean to me and wanted to give some of it back and maybe because I was a little frightened too, although I don't believe I knew of what. I hated myself for being so nasty to Donald.

"You're obviously in no mood to discuss this," he said.

I was about to remind Donald again that I was in mourning, and certainly in no frame of mind to chatter about what he called scholarship and what I—and any sane person—would call gossip. But something held me back—maybe it was a protective feeling. I couldn't forget what Royal Arsine had said about Donald, his suspicious accusations, which made me worry terribly about this sweet, brilliant man with his intelligent eyes and strokable hair. Also, there was a way Donald looked at me when he thought I didn't notice, and although I was a few years older, I could believe that he desired me, despite the possibility that he might be gay.

"I'm sorry if I sound impatient," I said. "A death in the family is very upsetting. I don't even know who should speak at the service."

"I imagine Roger will speak, and that might take care of it," Donald said. Then, after a short pause, he added, "I could speak if you wish."

I did not know how to respond to that offer. After all, it really wasn't my place to make that sort of commitment. As I considered all my obligations—all of the arrangements it had fallen to me to make—I felt an almost physical pressure squeezing my throat.

"If it had been my mother, I would have loved that," I finally said, which was a white lie. "And so would she," I added, compounding my thoughtful untruth.

At least we were no longer talking about Henrietta's hallucinations, although I was sure that the subject would come back in due course, as would everything else that had begun to make my life—so perfect until recently—so dreadfully complicated.

Twenty

✿

THE NEWS ABOUT HENRIETTA got around even before her obituary ("Mrs. Thrall Hopedale, Washington fixture, 88") appeared in the newspaper. But we live in a small town, as we often remind ourselves, and sometimes it feels like we've met every inhabitant more than once. Not that there aren't surprises. Just the other day, in fact, I discovered that Marlene De-Quella, my helper, was acquainted with a guest I'd never even heard of, a person who held a big job at the Department of Transportation. (To my astonishment, this man seemed genuinely interested in whiplash.)

Lots of people sent notes and called with condolences, which I know meant a lot to Roger. But there were some really strange calls too, like the one from Royal Arsine, who—and this may have been my imagination—was breathing heavily into the receiver, and not like he had a cold. The telephone rang at about eight in the morning (the truth is, he woke me), and I found it weird on almost every level.

"This must be terribly painful," he said.

"We're surviving it," I replied. "She had a full life."

I'm not an idiot, and I saw past the phoniness of this call, just as I had seen through Donald Frizzé's ploy: clearly, he wanted something. I noticed that Roger's side of the bed was deserted—perhaps, I thought, he was getting an early start on his so-called novel—and a moment later, I heard him making unpleasant noises in the bathroom.

"Are you alone?" Royal Arsine asked, and I looked around as if I'd somehow misplaced Roger. "I'd prefer to keep this call between us."

"I promise you he is not here at this moment and so our conversation, which will be very brief, is completely private. Shall I tell him you called?"

"Please don't," he said, in that mellow voice of his, which sounded much nicer when you couldn't see his face. "I imagine you'll have a big funeral. Thrall and Henrietta meant a lot to a certain generation in this town." He continued, "And you'll have lots of people over to the house—friends and such?"

I was puzzled by our dialogue and by the repeated manifestations of Royal Arsine, who seemed to be hinting that he wanted to take part in our family's ceremony of grief. I realize that I ought to have told Roger about my breakfast with Arsine, but I hadn't wanted to upset him. Now it suddenly seemed imperative to do so and, for that matter, to give a friendly heads-up to Donald Frizzé. The shower was running and I heard Roger groaning and sighing, which I'm sure was his way of coping with his sorrow, but when he came out of the bathroom I planned to act as if I hadn't heard a thing.

I'D ORIGINALLY TOLD ROGER that we should limit the guest list to a hundred, but it does add up fast. Most of Henrietta's friends have died or have moved into nursing homes, but just counting Roger's ex-wife and children and the people we absolutely had to invite—like anyone connected to Thrall—I realized that was too modest a number, even with no-shows. So I kept adding names. When I told Pete Plantain that I'd probably have to take the day off, he shrugged and said that Marlene could easily do the show alone, which gave me no choice: I invited Pete and Marlene to the funeral, and then I had to ask the weatherman, too.

Whatever we did, there were bound to be hurt feelings, which I think bothered me more than it did Roger, who barely listened whenever I suggested alterations to the master list. At least, as the day drew nigh, I got Roger to pay a little attention, and I think we arrived at a very good selection of men and women to celebrate Henrietta's rich life. We had three senators, five congressmen, two former cabinet officers, all of whom knew Thrall, and quite a few members of the press, who may want to write about Henrietta— that "end of an era" sort of story—and all kinds of people, active and retired, from the State Department. I'm very thrilled that we're also going to include some of the people who will be running this town for the next four years, maybe even the former president, and maybe someone from the brand-new cabinet. I don't think we'll have very many Clinton people, though.

A FEW DAYS BEFORE the funeral, my friend Jennifer Pouch called and for some reason began to talk about Royal Arsine, almost as if she knew it would get under my skin. "My sources tell me you had breakfast with him," she said, and laughed in a way she has when she thinks she knows something I don't.

"Jennifer," I replied, "in this case it's easy to know who your source is," and added, "Also, you were a little late to find out—it was ages ago."

She laughed self-consciously, and of course I should have known that Jennifer, who knows more people than anyone, was acquainted with Royal Arsine.

"We met when I was doing a story about a Soviet spy ring, back when we had Soviet spy rings," she said. "He was useful."

She must have been very young then, I thought, but didn't say it. I did say, "He seems like a sneak and also a weirdo."

"Well, maybe. Still, there are two things you should know, Trudy. One, Roy is going to get a very big job in the administration and that means they're willing to overlook a lot of what he did in the past." She paused. "Obviously, your husband knew him when he worked in the embassy and Roy—how shall I put it?— worked outside. Not as though Roger didn't know what he was up to."

I had no idea what she meant by that, and I was almost sorry that we'd invited Jennifer to the funeral and reception, although I knew she would never forgive me if she'd been left out. The last thing I needed was to alienate Jennifer Pouch.

"The other thing," she continued, "is Roy talks about you—he is very curious about our Trudy. Like I didn't know you danced in a bar in college." She paused, as if for effect, but I said nothing in reply and she started up again. "I know you think he's creepy, Trudy, but he's very interesting when you get to know him."

"He doesn't have any eyes," I said. "And he knows I'm happily married to Roger." Then I asked, "What big job is he getting?"

"Oh, you know, one of those intelligence things, I can't remember which, but it's huge and he'll be very important—he'll get face time with the president, which means a lot to him, because he's been out of it for eight years. Is *he* coming to the funeral?"

Of course we hadn't invited him, despite his hints the other morning it would have seemed absurd to both of us—and I had no idea how to get in touch with him even if we'd wanted to. But after my conversation with Jennifer, I began for the first time to consider it, and by late afternoon, I concluded that maybe Royal Arsine really did want to honor Henrietta's memory. Of course I hated the idea of asking him, but it wasn't my funeral—and this wasn't about me. And naturally there was a good chance that he wouldn't even see the invitation in time, since I had no idea where he actually lived. So I sent it by FedEx over to the Sturling Club, which I knew he frequented now and then, just like Roger. I should have asked Roger—I know that, I really do—but I honestly thought he wouldn't mind. And I never could have imagined the trouble it would cause.

Donald & Trudy

winter

Twenty-one
[Donald]

❧

I'VE BEGUN TO MAKE a fresh list of biographical prospects—vice presidents whose lives might reward even an impatient researcher—but it goes slowly, and my visits to the
Library are interrupted by the vibrations of my cell phone. These
are usually requests to appear on this or that television program,
although sometimes it is my friend Walter Listing, who will suggest a theatrical outing. Walter has tickets to a concert series at
the Kennedy Center as well as plays at the Folger, Arena Stage,
and other cultural diversions. (I realize that I haven't said much
about Walter, apart from noting that he's eager to resume his
career at the Pentagon, where he can make the most of his expertise in advanced weaponry, but he's a private person and genuinely hates the spotlight.)

Then I have those other distractions, such as Trudy's recent coldness. (I can never quite read Roger, although, for some reason, he has confided in me; he doesn't give much away, and I suspect there is not all that much to hide.) With Trudy, I don't know what it's about—her moods change by the hour—but I rather imagine she's annoyed by several things, including my lingering interest in Henrietta and my schedule, which doesn't allow me as much time to appear on her local program as I might wish. Maybe it was my imagination, but she seemed almost upset, perhaps even jealous, when I mentioned casually that I'd gotten a thoughtful, personal note from Vice President–elect Cheney's office. For some time, she has not been a happy camper.

I know that Henrietta's funeral was a great disappointment for Trudy. Of course lots of people who ought to have been there were already getting ready for the Inauguration, but there was nonetheless a noticeable absence of friends and officials; Henrietta did after all represent a vanishing generation in this town. (I suppose that we all take our turns vanishing, but an unhealthy emphasis on that existential view does not, I'm pretty sure, have much of a future in my field.) I could also sense Trudy's fury and mortification when she realized that no one from the television station, people she worked with every day, had bothered to come to the service or reception. I actually thought it was pretty well attended, and I was delighted to see any number of people I've come to know, including Senator Willingham, who sat near the back and left quickly, and a man from Henrietta's era, a former newspaper columnist named Brandon Sladder, who shows up on cable now and then (I can't bear the way his neck fat pushes his bow tie) and seems to be on his last legs. Sladder gave me a nod, as if we were old friends, and looked extremely pleased when I nodded back. There were also people like Gail Tachyon, the tense, plump real estate agent, who was eager to get the listing to Henrietta's Foggy Bottom apartment and to put it on the market while, as she whispered to Trudy, "its provenance is so fresh."

The funeral itself, though, was a sad affair. The sermon was uninspired and no one spoke particularly well, including Roger, who said that his mother had lived a full life, was devoted to her family, and all that. But his heart wasn't in it, and when everyone began to sing "A Mighty Fortress Is Our God," Roger appeared to be humming along, as if he had forgotten the words. I was particularly interested in how things would go with Roger's first wife and their two grown children (both, alas, had inherited the Hopedale nose), who sat across the aisle from Trudy and Roger and looked fiercely forward. I don't think the two women glanced at one another even once.

Louise is quite a few years older than Trudy, but she is attractive in a slim, winter-tanned, tennis-playing sort of way. We chatted briefly during the reception at the Hopedale house (we were both sipping warm white wine and reaching for cashews). I was delighted when she praised my work, even if she was referring to my television commentaries rather than to anything I've written. To establish my historian's credentials, I told her about Garret Augustus Hobart and his tenuous connection to the house in which we stood; she appeared fascinated when I described how the trail of our history might have veered had Hobart lived. I found that I liked Louise immensely, and our interesting conversation stopped only when Roger drifted over; he nodded gravely to me and planted a light kiss on Louise's cheek. Then Roger appeared almost to jump, as if startled by something, and right away I saw that he was looking toward the tiny dark eyes of that strange fellow Royal Arsine, who, ever since our curious election, seems to have acquired the habit of popping up whenever I least want to see him. I watched Arsine attempt an asymmetric grin as he approached us, walking, I noticed, a little duck-footed, and before his smile collapsed into a grimace and we were face to face, Roger had rushed off and Louise, with an expression of repugnance, as if she'd just swallowed something fetid, hurried in still another direction.

"Mr. Frizzé, we meet again," Arsine said, in a mock salute that he no doubt meant to be amusing.

"It's a company town," I replied, as he scratched his sprig of a mustache.

"I've heard you were close to Mrs. Hopedale in her last years," he said, moving closer and dropping his voice slightly.

I didn't much care for the way Arsine phrased that, as if he were implying something untoward, and I decided not to answer with more than a nod.

"And everyone," he went on, as a faint whiff of his breath puffed against me, "says that she was quite fond of you. Clearly, she confided in you as she did in few others, isn't that so?"

A Somalian waiter passed by, carrying tiny pizzas with olive bits in their center, and they looked so tasty that I reached for two. At least, I thought, Arsine wasn't about to torment me by once more bringing up the curious similarities between my pioneering study of Levi Morton and an ancient, forgotten attempt to tackle the same subject. "I don't believe in coincidence" was all he said about that, and because I feel much the same, I replied, "Me too— what a coincidence!"

I tried to swallow whole one of the miniature pizzas and covered my mouth when I realized that I'd overreached. The coin-sized snack burned the tender roof of my mouth, and as I spat it into my hand and tried to figure out what to do with this wasted food (which might have done some good in Somalia), I caught sight of Roger, his lips pressed against Trudy's ear. I could see from this short distance that his nostrils had widened, that his face was shockingly red, almost purple, and that he was pointing at Royal Arsine. My curiosity got the better of me, and as I drifted closer to them, I could hear him saying, "Damnit, Trudy, I don't ever want that fellow in my house!" When I looked at Arsine, I detected an embryonic smile under his snail-sized mustache, and as I turned my glance back toward Roger, I saw that his purplish face had gone so pale that even his hair appeared to lighten. Then I saw Arsine heading swiftly out the Hopedales' grand front door onto P Street, where cars were double-parked, and everyone standing in the foyer could feel the cold January air rushing in.

Twenty-two

❧

THERE ARE DAYS when I wish I'd never heard of Trudy Hopedale, much less become her close friend. Perhaps I don't really mean that; it's hard to imagine life in this town without Trudy and I know how much I owe her. But I also know how double-edged the Trudy sword is. My goodness, I'm no ingrate; thanks to my start on *Trudy's People* I've become famous in a low-key sort of way. But that doesn't win me the respect of my fellow historians or create the best environment for serious work. I was reminded of this on a recent Sunday, while reading about a new biography of Alben Barkley and, halfway through, suffering a brief bout of nausea. Alben Barkley! Hadn't I once thought that Barkley, the oldest of our vice presidents, would be a perfect subject for me? After all, the amusing word *veep* came into our language because Barkley's grandson could not pronounce the honorific, and, furthermore, people who had actually known him are still alive; Henrietta Hopedale certainly knew him. The reviewer was my onetime mentor, G. Buster Morgenmount, who seemed almost to be chiding me personally when he wrote that the author had "plowed a useful furrow in the rocky, unrewarding field of the vice presidency." I became increasingly depressed as I read his generous assessment for a second and third time, to the point where I could skip enviously over certain lines, such as "With this magisterial survey, one can finally put aside Barkley's own fascinating memoir, *That Reminds Me,* and be gratefully content." Such praise had the effect of making me even less eager to tackle my next subject, whoever that might turn out to be. How, I asked myself repeatedly, could I ever have shrugged off Barkley?

But back to Trudy: because of her, I met Jennifer Pouch, who thinks I'm a swine because I felt so little reciprocal attraction. (As I've noted, partially suppressed details about that night still leap into my thoughts: there was the moment when she paraded around her apartment wearing nothing but panties and a robe that she let swing open, as if by accident, and I recall her chunky legs crossing and uncrossing, as if speaking a desperate language of their own.) Jennifer, I've decided, is more or less untrustworthy; she may be a fine reporter, but she is one of those for whom the "story" is more important than the people in the story; she pretends to be sympathetic, but I know that it's a cold-blooded sympathy, the kind that wants to pry something out of you. And yes, I blame her for those rumors about me and Walter Listing, but people do love to talk about each other in this town.

Also, because of Trudy—or, more precisely, Roger—I have the

persistent Royal Arsine in my life. "You interest me," he said to me on the day of Henrietta's funeral, but I don't like being an object of his interest. I also can't imagine why he bothers with someone like me when he is close to getting one of the most important and powerful jobs in Washington or why he seems to take a curious pleasure in letting me know that he could impugn my scholarship and me along with it. It was all something of an unpleasant mystery, and the last time I looked at *Desks of Power*—before wrapping it carefully in brown paper for its final voyage back to the author—I found it hard to believe that Arsine saw it as a threat of some sort.

TRUDY, OF COURSE, has her own problems. I know she's been upset by the changes they're making to her program—we all find it hard to share. But now she thinks she's going to be fired, tossed away like some former officeholder. The last time she called, I was trying to read the paper (another story about our new president, who seems chock full of plans and looks wonderfully fit in his Wranglers) while also trying to listen to Bucky Ravenschlag's radio program, which, I have to confess, has become a persistent guilty pleasure. (Bucky Ravenschlag, in his nasal but somehow intelligent and compelling voice, was once more speaking unkindly, and with suspicion, about Hillary Clinton.) As I sped through an article about some energy calamity in California—it sounded horrible for those poor people—I tried to focus my attention on Trudy, who could barely speak between sobs, and I think my silent calm was helpful.

"I hate them, Donald!" she said. "They have no idea how valuable I am to them—what a mistake they're making by treating me this way."

When, after much of this, I finally suggested that leaving *Lunch with Marlene & Trudy,* as the program was now called, was not exactly a tragedy, she said, "I suppose you're right. My heart isn't in it. My heart isn't in much of anything these days." Then she broke into sobs again, saying, "They'll call it *Marlene's People*—I can't bear that—that's *my* name!"

But there was clearly more to her misery than the loss of her noontime forum. There was also Roger, of whom she said, "I can't tell you how strange he's been. He's crazed because that spooky Royal Arsine came to the house after the funeral—'sneaking around,' he keeps saying. He blames me for that."

"But Trudy," I pointed out, "I believe it was you who invited him."

She ignored that and added, "And I suppose you know that Royal Arsine seems to have a fixation on *you*."

My heart stopped at Trudy's use of the word "fixation"—an ominous step up from "interest." It occurred to me that much of our country's recent history has been determined by the fixation of one person, or group, upon another. I jotted a quick note to myself ("history as fixation") while Trudy continued to ramble on about the minor episodes that lent pathos to her life and about her little dilemmas, such as whether or not to go forward with another three-table dinner party. I would never use the word "shallow" to describe Trudy, whom I adore, but sometimes she does seem a little small-minded. *Fixation.* As I worried anew about Arsine and his interest in what was no more than a small ethical lapse when I was a youthful scholar, I could imagine my own life—a model on its surface—taking a bad turn. I was barely paying attention when Trudy mentioned, almost in passing, that Jennifer Pouch had been telling people I was not a wholly normal man. I felt for the first time like an outsider. At least, I told myself, I was not guilty of producing anything like *Desks of Power.* The thought comforted me. For the last time, I undid my careful wrapping and turned to it—hoping that each fresh page would appall me.

. . . Mitch MacPeters's prick tingled from Tammy Roberts's nearness, her flowery smell, and as soon as she had closed the great oaken door of his office and left, he got to work. He was grateful for his physical condition, and it did not take him long to stuff The Interrogator into a dark green trash bag, either a Hefty or a Glad, one of those widely advertised as being able to hold large loads. MacPeters was impressed by the way the sack stretched and bulged, yet remained intact, but the insertion was still hard work and he was breathing heavily when he knotted it shut with the convenient handle ties at the top. Then he dragged the load through his imposing outer door and left it in the silent corridor, to be carted away by the maintenance crew.

By this time, the senator felt less fearful. He had managed to persuade himself that a trash bag with this bulk need not arouse suspicion, perhaps because he'd pasted a note to the outside saying, "Sensitive papers and discarded amendments to bills; please destroy." But his hands trembled nonetheless whenever he heard sounds, even faint ones, like mousy putterings. When he heard the muted clatter of Tammy Roberts's delicate knuckles on the door to his private office, he was grateful that she hadn't left him in the lurch.

"You're still here," he observed.

She gave him an unfathomable smile and said, "I almost helped you carry out the trash."

"It's been a very hard day."

Suddenly, without a word, her right hand unbuckled his Italian calfskin belt, which persuaded him that it was permissible to unbutton her crisp cotton blouse. Her scented breasts, sweetly embroidered with the tracings of bluish veins, quivered as he bent to kiss the first and then the second, circling each wrinkly orange nipple with his tongue and noticing that they were not perfectly matched. "Senator MacPeters," she said, sliding under his embrace. "Mitch," he replied. She removed the rest of her garments and stood by his venerable desk in all of her modest, dappled nakedness, girlish and ripe, her sweet darknesses so unlike the drooping, sad, almost dusty form of Tootsie, his wife.

For the next few minutes, MacPeters put aside everything that had been weighing on his thoughts. He forgot about the green trash bag, the controversial bill on pesticides (S.4006-b) he had championed against the forces of money and corruption, the possibility of having to run against that former Green Bay Packer, his marriage to Tootsie, who had become almost a stranger to him, his hallucinating mother, beset by endless erotic fantasies, and even the pressure to confirm the corrupt and vengeful Tony Snike as the nation's next intelligence chief. He wanted to reveal Snike's past to the newspapers, although that brought with it the risk of revealing his own, extremely minor, role in Snike's past. Tammy played with his swollen cock, and then her lips found their tumescent, purple prey; a moment later, they tumbled to the floor, his head bumping against the side of his desk as her milky, fleshy thighs parted in the ultimate gesture of welcome.

In the minutes that remained until they merged, he finding her dark suppleness, she finding his, the senator could not argue, nor did he wish to. But then he could not forget the papery face of the dead Interrogator. Finding the body, he was now positive, was a warning not to hurt Snike's chances. The thought of Snike, with his little mustache and charming demeanor, made him despair. Tammy's vibrant pussy closing around his engorged cock gave him solace momentarily, but soon his past began to batter . . .

I smiled. I had to wonder if my dear friend Trudy, who's been sounding so downcast and worried of late, had seen any of this and, if so, what she might think.

Twenty-three
[Trudy]

✿

I HAVE TRIED, really tried hard, to enjoy another Washington spring. The tulips are out, the cherry blossoms have come and gone, and the awful summer—everyone sweating and complaining—still seems far away. But it is hard to relax when the telephone keeps ringing and you find yourself talking to people you don't want to. Like my good friend Jennifer Pouch, who wanted to tell me about a man she's dating, a person ten years younger—"He's so vigorous, Trudy, if you know what I mean"—and she was probably offended when I didn't ask her any questions about this outstanding person. Do I sound sarcastic? Why don't I care? All I could think about were my aforementioned problems, of which there are more every day, starting with Roger. It feels like all he has done since his mother died is mope, unless he's working on that hideously embarrassing book. I think he really expected someone to ask him to join the administration, and what makes it so sad is that Roger has no idea how ridiculous he appears to these Bush people—showing up at things with his striped ties and that fancy East Coast accent. I think he should have gotten the hint when we were totally left out of the Inaugural festivities, every one of them. Sometimes I have no idea why I married Roger, although of course I don't mean that. I love him, although I might not marry him today if I had it to do over.

Not that I'm doing much better. Thanks to Pete Plantain, I am definitely being pushed off my own program. When Pete and Marlene DeQuella didn't have the simple courtesy to be there for my mother-in-law's funeral, they couldn't have sent a clearer signal. At least Marlene had the grace to apologize in her phony way, shaking her head and saying that she had gotten a really rotten cold and didn't want to spread her little germs among the mourners. I've also noticed that Pete just about ignores any suggestion I make about who to have on my program, and so we ask people like that woman who collects old hubcaps and that retarded-looking man from the Internal Revenue Service. At least we still book Donald Frizzé when he's free, but that's because Marlene still has a great big crush on him. Which won't get her anywhere at all.

I hadn't given Royal Arsine much thought apart from following his reborn career, so I must say I was surprised when he showed up at the door one warm morning in May. There are some people you grow to dislike and some who never seem very likable, but then there are those you hate on sight—who make you feel a little less sympathetic toward the entire human race—and he must have seen how unwelcome he was by the look on my face, as if he knew how he'd ruined the reception after Henrietta's funeral. I've never seen Roger so angry and upset, the way he scolded me in front of everyone, including his ex-wife, who must have really enjoyed that spectacle. Even before all the mourners left, Roger had turned completely unreasonable, as if it was entirely my fault.

"Roger's not home," I said to Royal Arsine.

"Believe me, I know that," he said, and of course I understood right away that he knew a lot about our daily habits, as if he'd been watching the house or something. He added, "I'll be just a minute." He raised his right hand as if he was taking an oath.

Even though the day was warm, he wore a dark suit and perspiration flattened his little mustache. His white shirt looked too tight, and I could pity his raw neck if not him.

"It can't be more than a minute because I have to go to work," I informed him.

"Your show?" He bowed his head and made the sign of the cross as if that was supposed to be funny.

I searched his minute eyes for a sign of human life, and finding none, I looked at his mouth, which seemed to have shrunk since the last time I'd seen him. I chose to ignore his last insinuation and stepped outside to make clear my determination not to linger.

"You think I'm a pest," he said, and presented one of his frightening smiles, the one that made his mouth turn sideways. "You think I ask too many questions about your husband and your friend Donald, the would-be historian."

"You have no idea what I think," I said, trying not to show my impatience.

"The only person I haven't asked you about is the senator—Willingham I think it was," he said, and I began to notice how he had this sickeningly formal way of putting things in his refined voice. "Of course it's none of my business with whom you choose to commit your adulteries."

Was this man judging me—or, even worse, threatening to tell Roger? I was ready to cry and I wanted to slam the door in his face, but he smiled aslant again and just looked at me like I was some sort of specimen or something. And I looked back at him as if I didn't care.

"I can't imagine what you're implying, Mr. Arsine—"

"Roy."

"Well, I can't imagine."

"By the way," he said, "I have a few pictures from the days when you danced in Ann Arbor."

"So do I," I replied haughtily.

My next-door neighbor, a retired budget analyst with long gray hair that he'd fashioned into a ponytail, was walking his dog, a handsome poodle. He stopped to stare, as if something might be wrong, and I realized that Royal Arsine in his dark suit and white shirt looked like a federal agent of some sort. So I waved at my neighbor and I changed the subject.

"It's all about what you and Roger did in Central America or someplace like that, isn't it?"

I was thrilled to see from his expression (his eyes almost disappeared) that my question was unwelcome.

"Look, Trudy," he said, lifting an arm and resting a hand gently on my shoulder. "It might be better if we could talk privately." His hand felt frosty, even on this spring day—even through the cloth of my blouse—and I removed it quickly, gripping it by his long, calloused thumb, trying not to touch his fingernails. I recalled Jennifer's theory that this revolting man might want to have sex with me.

Then he muscled his way into the foyer, which opened to our living room on the left and, on the right, the dining room where Roger and I had given so many memorable dinners. I told myself that this was as close as Mr. Royal Arsine was ever going to get to actual Hopedale hospitality, even if he got that fabulous job people were talking about. I realized that I wasn't quite sure where Roger was and that he might return at any moment; the last time I'd seen him was before breakfast, when he had been brushing his teeth with the toothbrush that sounded like a motorboat.

Before I could object, Royal Arsine headed for the living room, sat on our off-white sofa, which we'd recently purchased, and crossed his legs, revealing a brand-new pair of tan cowboy boots with extremely pointed toes and all that detail that they call hand-tooling. I couldn't help noticing that an oblong chunk of what appeared to be dog poo was hanging from the sole of one boot; the boot was suspended over one of our Persian rugs, and I considered going to fetch a newspaper. Then he crossed his leg the other way, and it was too late for that.

"I've never understood what it is you want from me," I said.

He seemed to be grinding his shoe into the rug, but that could have been my imagination.

"It's simple," he replied. "There's a job I very much want." He paused and added, "I need to be confirmed and your husband could make that more difficult. As you may guess, I once did things I now regret . . ."

I was studying the ugly new spot on the rug when I realized that he hadn't quite finished his sentence. All I could think to say was "We all hate difficulty." Then, when he didn't respond, I added, "And we all have regrets."

That off-kilter smile of his appeared again as he ignored my observation and in that resonant voice he said, "And I think you understand how I could embarrass *you*."

When I laughed politely, he gave me a crafty look. Not for the first time, I wondered what this man had done and what Roger knew about it—or might have done himself. One thing about Washington, I've learned over the years, is that the place really is filled with secrets and also that no one keeps them very well or for very long. Not that many secrets are all that interesting, but some of them are pretty awful and a few of them are the sort you wish you never learned about in the first place.

Twenty-four

❧

I MUST HAVE SOUNDED hysterical when I called Donald Frizzé. I mean I just lost control, and because I trusted Donald, I probably said things I shouldn't have. I told him that I'd been screwing Ricardo Willingham—"Well, letting him screw me," I said, "past tense"—which I suspect he knew, but I also wanted him to know that people were saying that his work wasn't all that original.

"People like to say hurtful things about other people" was all he said, and he accompanied that with a little chuckle that I couldn't interpret and added, "But listen, Trudy, I'm actually very busy."

I knew he was lying and I became very irritated at his smug tone, like he was on some television panel and acting like he knew everything and none of this was bothering him. But Donald actually has a very unsophisticated idea of how Washington works and I really believe he wouldn't understand much about anything if it hadn't been for me. Also, it's like he doesn't get how important it is to stand by old friends. It's hard to describe the despair I was suddenly experiencing, a feeling that my life was about to turn inside out or upside down, and the next thing I knew I heard myself saying something that surprised me after I'd said it: "I don't think I want to have Fourth of July this year."

I thought I heard Donald gasp, and he reminded me that I didn't have it last year, either, which I certainly knew better than him.

"Well, maybe I'm sick of our silly barbecue," I said, although I suppose I didn't really mean it. "Maybe I'm sick of the disgusting pig we cook and the porky smells and the garbage on the lawn and the pee on the floor of our private upstairs bathroom, even though we tell people to use the one downstairs."

"You could lock your bathroom door," Donald said in the same smug tone, as if the pee on the floor was what was really bothering me.

"Also, everyone knows I'm being fired and they'll feel sorry for me. I hate pity."

"No one thinks it's your fault," Donald said. "How could they?"

"It's not a question of my fault!" I replied in a loud voice. "It's about loyalty."

"Your friends are loyal to you, Trudy," he said in that really annoying self-satisfied voice.

Of course I couldn't call off July 4th—not with the guest list almost complete (a good one too, I thought) and our big deposit already cashed by the catering service. So I said, "I know people count on me. It's like summer isn't the same without it."

"That's the spirit, kid," Donald said, and I could have killed him.

I didn't need to say that this year's barbecue was going to be our first formal hello to the Bush administration, a gracious, personal welcome for people we've never met and a way to get reacquainted with all the others—many of them friends—that we used to know. Even if more than a few of my acquaintances are sure they stole the election, a lot of us think it's time to put all that bitterness behind us and look ahead, to show some hospitality and leave partisanship back at the office. After all, didn't Jack Kennedy steal his election, and doesn't this sort of thing happen all the time? Also, it's not as though they personally stole it or that anything was going to change if everyone stayed so mad, or that they were going to vanish for the next four years. Naturally I understand why some people are so furious, but there are amazing men and women in both parties who only want what's best for the country. Deep down, I really believe that. Or I think I do.

"You just have to calm down and be yourself," Donald said when I didn't answer him, and his voice by now had gotten so patronizing and syrupy that I slammed down the phone, as I've done before with Donald even though he's one of my closest friends.

ANYWAY, I FELT LIKE I was going crazy and probably for no good reason. I had no idea anymore what was going on in the world, the news was all so depressing. One morning I read how the entire royal family of Nepal was massacred, and on another day Bush people began to accuse Clinton people of vandalizing the White House—it was so petty—and it seemed like every hour someone used the word "bloodshed" (I absolutely *hate* that word!) even though there seems to be more and more of it. When I called my mom (I've actually been calling her a lot since Henrietta left us), she said that there's been a lot of bloodshed in Detroit too, and pretty soon I changed the subject and heard myself talking about buying another new sofa to replace the one that Royal Arsine had used, and a rug too. But then she was telling me how the school where she'd taught was being closed and pretty soon both of us were crying. I know that people would laugh at me if I ever said how much I missed having my mom close by. At my age!

I THINK I'M ACTUALLY glad about leaving my stupid show, and at first I didn't even notice how hyper Roger had become, the way he was going out for walks late at night and had started talking to himself. Roger and I weren't speaking much—not out of hostility but because our minds were elsewhere. At night, he always manages to fall asleep when I'm brushing my teeth. It's like he's losing all his remaining appetite for sex, except when he writes about it. He doesn't even bother to look up when I put on my black Victoria's Secret peekaboo slip and walk around the bedroom. In fact Roger hasn't seemed the least bit interested in anything that interests me, and one day in June I tested him by saying what I'd said to Donald: that I'd just as soon call off the barbecue. Roger barely looked up when I made my little announcement. Instead, he smiled in a slow sort of way, nodded his head until the ripples in his hair began to shake, and finally said, "Not a bad idea, Trudy."

"You're not serious," I replied, and I could see that our little discussion had become a puzzlement to him.

"Just think of all the people we won't have to see," he said, and went on to mention a few men and women that, I have to admit, I wasn't all that crazy about myself.

Then he suddenly changed the subject and said, "I have this feeling that my manuscript has been read by strangers."

Was Roger accusing me? It was hard to read his expression, especially when he lifted his chin and those wide nostrils of his seemed like they were staring at me.

"I haven't heard a thing," I replied, truthfully.

"If so," Roger said, "then the cat's out of the bag, the horse is out of the barn, and the car is racing down the highway."

"You make it sound so dramatic," I said, with a little giggle, and Roger stared at me in that accusing, unfair way he sometimes has.

"If you cancel the barbecue, you'd better hurry up," he replied.

"If it's not too late, I just might," I said, and of course he knew that I was bluffing, just as I knew that he really didn't care either way.

Twenty-five

I COULDN'T DO IT—canceling our Fourth of July bash would be like completely giving up on everything but my heart wasn't in it, not even when the truck began to unload and I saw the long tables and the red, white, and blue bunting piling up on our back lawn. When Roger saw the truck, he shook his head and, without a word, went out for a walk. He didn't come back until I'd seen to all the preparations and was totally exhausted, but I felt myself reviving as the hour approached and the light in the sky, ever so slightly, began to fade.

Some things are the same every year. For instance, someone always tries to crash our party, and usually we find a polite way to ask the person to please leave. We feel sorry for them—there are so many hurt feelings, especially from people we've had to drop from the list, like Gail Tachyon, who's put on some weight and gotten so pushy about her listings—but as a practical matter, the belt cannot expand to fit everyone. Once in a while, though, we have wonderful surprises, like when someone really special suddenly appears, and I was so pleased when I spotted Bucky Ravenschlag, a man I certainly didn't know personally. But at about seven o'clock, there he was, Bucky Ravenschlag himself, rolling across the lawn in his fancy wheelchair, smoking a cigar, even though Roger and I have forbidden smoking in our house and on our grounds. I knew right away who it was because I don't know anyone who uses a wheelchair. Plus he wore a baseball cap that said "I ♥ Bucky," and I don't think I know anyone who wears baseball caps, either. He knew who I was too, and he wheeled himself to my side and began to speak in the fast, high-pitched nasal voice he uses on the radio, which I guess is his real voice.

"Hope you don't mind my stopping by, Mrs. Hopedale, but I happened to be in the neighborhood," he said, with a huge smile and a shy expression that I have to admit I found charming.

"Please call me Trudy," I replied, and took his extended hand, surprised by his thin, delicate fingers. He looked much younger than I had expected. His face was pink and beardless, and his blond hair looked like it was thinning rapidly. And let me say right here that I don't endorse a lot of what Bucky says when he's on the radio, like this idea that Hillary Clinton killed somebody in Arkansas, and also the other stuff.

I stopped one of our waiters, a tall Arab-looking man in a white robe, and asked him to please bring some food for our new arrival. Bucky looked grateful, and within moments, we were surrounded by other guests, including my good friend Jennifer Pouch, who knows that my parties are off-the-record, even though she's such a good reporter. I didn't realize until that moment how many people knew who Bucky was, and I was a little taken aback at the way Jennifer, who was wearing an extremely loose-fitting black and white summer dress, gushed all over him, as if he was the most important person there. She kept talking even when Bucky began to dig into his ham and coleslaw and potato salad, eating so fast that I don't know how he caught his breath.

"I just love your program," Jennifer was saying, leaning over him and exposing just about everything above the waist. "I don't know how you do it every day—just talk and talk, as if there's no limit to what you've stored up in your little brain."

Bucky should have been flattered, but something she said, or maybe it was the way she said it, annoyed him, and when he'd finished his food, he held up his empty plate for more. I guessed Jennifer was hovering because she was dying to be on Bucky's program like lots of her journalist friends, but I could tell from Bucky's expression that this was never going to happen. A few minutes later, when Jennifer went to another part of the lawn, there was Donald Frizzé, and Bucky seemed to know who he was too, probably from television. "Greetings, Mr. Historian!" Bucky said. "Why don't you come on the show?" and I watched Donald almost gratefully grab Bucky's outstretched hand while a waiter replaced his empty plate with a full one, setting it down carefully on Bucky's tray. It was a memorable sight: Donald, with his thick hair and gorgeous smile, his lean athletic body (he was wearing a new faded red polo shirt and crisp khakis), leaning to speak to the little man in his chair, who was crumpled up like a living pillow. Bucky looked relaxed, and I just hoped he wouldn't start talking about moral clarity and good and evil, and all that, which made him sound smug, as if he alone had been chosen to represent the right side. I always had the feeling that his lip curled when he said that sort of thing, which is why he was better on the radio.

To my surprise, the party I'd almost called off was turning into a glorious evening as the dull brightness of the late afternoon sky began to fade. An excellent assortment of guests had shown up, and I thought that Roger and I had done pretty well after all. I saw two of George W. Bush's cabinet appointments, quite a few congressmen, and lots of the people who make Washington so unique, including the chairman of the FCC and, although it wasn't actually him, as it turned out, someone who looked just like Alan Greenspan. Of course there were the people I had to invite, like Senator Willingham, who stared at my pink blouse, which Roger said was too tight but which I thought was designed perfectly for my upper body. (I couldn't imagine how I could ever have had anything to do with Ricardo, and all I could remember was the way he had grunted and groaned and rubbed his stubbly face against me.) Roger was nice enough to invite some people who were once famous, like that broken-down former columnist Brandon Sladder, and some friends from the old State Department who knew Thrall and Henrietta and whose names I could never remember. Of course there was no one from the television station. I hope they're satisfied with their plans for the fall; I doubt that anyone else will be. I don't know anyone who watches my program now.

The only person I definitely didn't want to see was Royal Arsine, who has pretty much disappeared since he began his new job. It looked for a day or two like the Senate wouldn't confirm him—the newspaper had a story about a "surprise witness" and there were rumors about certain unspeakable activities overseas—but no one said any more than that and I realized that Royal was now exceedingly powerful; maybe I should have been nicer to him, but I always hated the idea of being nice to someone I loathe and detest because they're important. At just the thought of him, I looked around, almost panicked, to be doubly sure he wasn't there; it was getting darker and harder even to recognize people I did know.

Someone waved and I waved back, realizing it was Donald Frizzé circling the lawn. When all is said and done, Donald is as big a mystery to me as anyone. I've never understood why he's so interested in all those dead people who used to live in our town and why he wants to write books nobody will ever buy or read. I would think he'd care more about living people. And just as I expected, he showed up alone, although almost any woman I know would have loved to be his guest. I told him to bring along Walter Listing, and he seemed offended at the suggestion. This town is too small sometimes, that's for sure.

☙

As it got seriously dark—it must have been close to ten o'clock and the musicians we'd hired had started to make spurting sounds on their horns—and as the smoke and porky fumes were getting pretty intense, I found myself once more standing next to Bucky Ravenschlag, whose wheelchair had glided up beside me. His pink cheeks looked a little flushed, and now I could see that his hair was so thin he looked bald. It was hard to imagine that more than four million people listened to every word this person uttered, but I also have to say that something about him was pretty compelling.

"Take my hand," he said, and when I did, his other hand began to stroke my buttocks.

"Look, Bucky," I said, "this is very gratifying but entirely inappropriate." I was glad that his groping, which was not altogether unpleasant, could not be easily detected in the deep twilight.

"You make me hot," he said.

"Bucky, stop it!" I replied. "You just can't do that to someone without asking."

"Sorry, Mrs. Hopedale," he said, and he looked absolutely crestfallen. He leaned against his cushions, like some sort of tiny pasha, and sighed, saying, "Just seeing you makes me almost explode." He pointed to his lap, and at what appeared to be an erection out of proportion to his size.

I began almost to like Bucky (who can resist that sort of preposterous flattery?) and wanted to ask his opinion about all sorts of things that were going on, like the FBI agent who was going to jail for being a Russian spy, and what should happen to that man Milosevic at his war-crimes trial, and all that. I wondered if maybe he would want me on his show and smiled at just the thought of how jealous Jennifer Pouch would be. But there was too much noise and commotion to have a proper conversation, and after I forcibly removed Bucky's hand, which had a powerful grip on a sensitive part of me, he seemed less eager to talk. The guests, shadows and solids, were milling about and going back to the buffet tables for seconds and thirds, and in the distance, you could hear the pops of neighborhood fireworks, the occasional cherry bomb and little rockets being launched from nearby lawns. It was magical, although the noises filling the dim streets of Georgetown made me a little jumpy, and more eager to see the magnificent display by the Monument. And it was almost time for Roger and me to lead the march around the lawn.

I saw Donald Frizzé and Jennifer Pouch standing close to me, and in the vanished light, it looked like their conversation was not all that friendly, not the way their arms were waving. The waving continued, and when my curiosity got the better of me, I patted Bucky's hair and headed their way, as fast as I could discreetly walk. As I got within earshot I heard the phrases "stealing his work" and "please don't!" and then Donald was shaking his head; he walked away swiftly, looking angry, then for some reason he was leaning over my rosebushes. When Jennifer caught sight of me, she turned and pretended not to see me, and after I just stared at her, she hurried off to be sure we didn't have to talk. Then I somehow found myself next to Bucky, who once more had wheeled to my side and was still attracting a curious crowd.

"Glad you're back, Mrs. Hopedale," Bucky said, pointing once more to the growth of his lap.

"Stop it, Bucky," I said, but I couldn't help smiling as I said it, and I saw Ricardo Willingham walking our way, wobbling as if he'd had a bit too much to drink. I dreaded what would happen next—that Ricardo would act a little too familiar. And then he did.

"Ah, my sweet potato!" he said, like W. C. Fields, but of course what he really wanted was to meet the famous Bucky Ravenschlag. To Bucky, he said, "I'm Senator Willingham."

"I know who you are," Bucky said, and he seemed to go more into his nasal radio voice. "I don't want to sound impolite at Mrs. Hopedale's wonderful party, but I've wondered why you always seem to vote for any bill that makes our nation a little weaker—like you expect our enemies, who are very evil people, to make nice when we roll over." Then his upper lip did curl, just like I imagined it would. "Those people hate us and they aren't nice."

"Now wait just a minute," Ricardo said, looking about as surprised as I'd ever seen him.

But Bucky was in no mood to converse. He took my hand once more, squeezed it tight, and rolled toward the edge of the lawn, where two men I didn't know wheeled him away into the summer night. A little later, the fireworks went up, and the band played Sousa and we marched around the lawn feeling proud and very American, and I said to myself, and later to Roger, that it was the best party we'd ever had. Roger, though, wasn't paying attention to the explosions of red and blue fire overhead and didn't seem to care what I thought. "Someone broke into my office," he said, and at first I thought I had misunderstood. But when I looked again at my husband, I saw that the man who moments before had been slapping people on the back and high-stepping to Sousa and enjoying our special night looked as whitish as death.

Twenty-six
[Donald]

M Y FRIEND WALTER LISTING advises me not to
worry so much, especially now that it's August and everyone is away. But I do tend to fret over my own welfare, and to be
honest, Walter seems disconcertingly indifferent to my dicey situation, no doubt because he's thrilled, and rightly so, about return-
ing to his desk at the Pentagon. Unlike Walter, though, I don't
really have a job, but rather a reputation of sorts, and I know how
fragile reputations in this town can be. People rise and fall, and
usually they don't rise again.

My producer at CBS wants me to opine about that congressman everyone is talking about, the fellow who may have had
sexual intercourse with an intern who's gone missing. Fascinating,
I suppose, but that's not my field of expertise and I don't think I'm

quite up for improvising—I might as well be asked about the shark attacks in Florida. People have sexual relations and sharks attack— people fuck and sharks bite, I was about to say with uncharacteristic sarcasm—and that's the way of the world. But I'm trying to hide the funk I've been in since the Hopedale barbecue, which was one of the worst social experiences of my life. Although it's been more than a month, I still think about it and wait for the other shoe (the one that Walter Listing shrugs off) to plop down on my head.

If one single thing ruined it for me (though it was more than one thing), it was my conversation with Jennifer Pouch. Of course I respect Jennifer as a journalist and she can be very entertaining, but there is something a little pathetic, even desperate, about her; that's definitely the way she seemed during our one short evening out. Trudy's theory is that Jennifer feels let down by life itself because she's unfulfilled as a woman. I can't judge such things (I'm not a woman), but I can't deny that Jennifer made me awfully uncomfortable when she headed my way on that muggy Fourth of July, trailed by a cloud of gnats. Like everyone, she was carrying a cardboard plate filled to overflowing with barbecued ribs and coleslaw (a rust-colored dab of sauce clung to her nose), and then, right to my face, she brought up the calumny that's been whispered behind my back: that I was a habitual plagiarizer, from my youthful (some would say precocious) senior thesis on John Nance Garner to my acclaimed study of Levi Morton. She did it with a sneaky smile that she probably thought was charming, saying, "Donald, I can't believe this, and I hate even to say it, but I've heard," and so on, and we both knew what she was up to.

"I've heard those allegations too," I said, "and I'm pretty tired of them. Also, is this the time or place to bring that up?"

"I notice you didn't deny it," she replied between bites, burrowing in like some amateur DA.

I hastened to repair my response.

"People repeat outrageous lies," I said, hoping that would do the trick.

"Sometimes," Jennifer said, chewing a little too loudly, *smack-smack,* "the lies are true. That's what makes gossip and rumor and innuendo so interesting." *Smack-smack.*

I noticed that she licked her lips when uttering the word "innuendo," and that she tilted her head and gave me what I suppose was meant to be a flirtatious look. As I say, I now and then recall bits from our single outing—our "date"—but the sight of her always had the effect of making me recall more minutiae about that particular night. And this being Washington, I seem to run into her all the time. In fact, I run into everyone all the time. I suppose it was rude of me to slap her hand when she attempted to touch my trousers near the spot that shielded my privates, but if I hadn't done so, it might only have led to more attempted intimacies and greater mutual embarrassment. (I may also have said to her, "There's a good reason they call them 'privates.'") I know that deep down she saw that response as a form of total rejection.

Needless to say, I found it disturbing to hear that my alleged transgressions had become conversational currency. It was bad enough when Royal Arsine muttered his suspicions, but far worse when they were repeated by a reporter who had the power to ruin me. The furious joy I began to see in her ever-shifting, eye-batting expression was baffling, and I realized that I needed to do more than simply deny it. So I rested my hand on Jennifer's bare shoulder, and while I took no pleasure in this contact with her slightly damp skin, I stroked gently, pausing by her clavicle while she gnawed the ribs, *smack-smack*. After a moment, the chewing stopped and she looked at me with surprise and, I think, some gratitude.

"I love this sort of night," she said, as I explored her uninteresting shoulder. From around the sloping lawn, one could hear fragments of conversation filled with phrases like "tasking the agency" and "implement a robust policy," and now and then a mosquito made for the back of my neck, my swats not always arriving in time to foil their missions, and I had to wonder if this season's bites would inject me with the West Nile encephalitis that I narrowly escaped a year ago. I smiled (my smile had more than once been called "dazzling"), and to Jennifer, I observed, "Isn't it amazing that the most powerful people in the world"—I extended my arm and made a sweeping motion—"can enjoy a simple backyard picnic?"

Jennifer nodded at that, glancing over toward Bucky Ravenschlag, with whom we had both conversed, and we spotted quite a few men and women whose faces would instantly be recognized by the most casual follower of events—people, I've discovered, who are in most ways just like you and me. I thought, as I often had, how lucky I was to be in this place at this time, and yet how fragile my grip on it felt. On one level, my actual culpability amounted to little more than the careless borrowing of some paragraphs—a few pages at most—and the judicious use of some helpful footnotes and interpretations. But I wasn't naïve: I could see how people who did not wish me well could use this to hurt me. And I needed to know how far the story had traveled. If it was widespread, I realized, I might have to retreat from my visible life, perhaps even leave town temporarily, although I could not quite imagine where I would go or what I would do when I got there. I didn't care if no one asked me back to *Marlene's People*—Marlene DeQuella herself was a little overblown—but I wondered if CBS would drop me and hire someone like the fellow who wrote that new book about Alben Barkley.

My fingers were getting a little tired of Jennifer's moist shoulder, but I didn't want to send the wrong signal by removing them. I thought of switching arms, but that might seem too calculated, and so I had the idea of asking for a bite of her food.

"That coleslaw looks magnificent," I said.

"It's the best," she replied, and finished off every scrap of it, *smack-smack*, mixing the creamy cabbage bits in with the last shred of dark pulled pork. Then she added, "So tell me, Donald: why do you think people are saying that about you? Do you think they're making it up?"

At that, I finally liberated my hand and tried to match her friendly, teasing expression, managing a twinkle in my eye and a reciprocal tilt of my head. I shrugged and said, "People like to say whatever makes them sound interesting."

If that didn't satisfy her (she had a quizzical expression), the conversation ended when a chubby fellow who once did something vital in Clinton's White House joined us. The man, who wore a ridiculous multicolored shirt and baggy jeans, planted kisses on both of Jennifer's cheeks and greeted me as if we knew each other. His name escaped me, but I remembered him from the impeachment circus three years ago (it already felt like the distant past) and how he'd looked as if he was about to die of exhaustion. It made me feel a little rotten for having been so amused by the scandal.

"Is that really Bucky Ravenschlag?" the chubby man asked us with a shake of his head, and we turned to watch the famous radio talk-show host wheeling across the lawn. I now remembered that the fat man (I noticed that he had pale, thin arms that looked unused) once worked for the National Security Council, and he shook his head again, as if he'd just remembered some of Bucky's boldest assertions. Then he looked right at me and said, "I just heard something about *you*, Don, but I can't remember what." Then he stopped himself as if he did remember and didn't want to say it. I could imagine.

"It's an awful thing to watch when someone gets destroyed in this town," Jennifer said, presenting the chubby man with one of her enigmatic smiles.

By now, I was feeling queasy, as if I were back in college and Professor Morgenmount was about to give a decisive exam on a subject I hadn't prepared for. Just as I was about to break up our chatty trio, I was rescued by Roger Hopedale, who strolled over, spreading his arms in welcome, as if imitating an airplane ready to land. After the usual greetings and kisses, he pulled me off to the side, saying to Jennifer and the man in big dungarees, "Sorry, but I need to speak to our young friend alone."

As soon as we were several steps away, Roger's face changed.

The benign indifference of the perfect host was replaced by the fierce worry of a man in torment. "Tell me," he said, "what you've done with my manuscript."

I certainly wasn't going to admit that *Desks of Power* had returned to the bottom of my coat closet, where it needed to be rewrapped after picking up fresh water from discarded umbrellas. I couldn't remember what I'd told him, in fact, and it was hard to keep track of all my stories. This was yet another reminder that I ought to keep notes on my own conversations.

"I know I meant to return it after enjoying it," I said, and asked, "Is something wrong?"

Roger, to use one of my favorite phrases, looked stricken.

"I wish I'd never written a word," he said. "It cuts too close to the bone."

"It's just a yarn, isn't it?" I asked.

"It's more complicated," he said. "Perhaps the easiest thing is for you to destroy your copy."

That, I assured him, would be no problem, but my words didn't seem to alleviate his nervousness, which was beginning to affect me too. My queasiness was evolving into full-fledged nausea, and at that moment there was nothing I wanted more than to be on my way. The angle of Roger's head emphasized the snoutlike features of his nose, and I smelled the sharp odor of barbecue when he put his hand on my arm and, leaning close, said, "Donald, as a friend, I also have to tell you that I've been hearing disturbing stories about you. I pray they're not true."

"I have the same prayers," I replied.

A little later, I realized that my response hadn't sounded quite right, but there had been no time to choose my words more carefully. The retired military musicians had begun to assemble and puff on their trumpets, trombones, and tubas, readying themselves for Sousa, and by then I felt so wretched that I dashed off, not feeling able to take part in the little parade around the grounds, the one that was always led by Trudy and Roger. No doubt several people saw me throwing up onto one of the Hopedales' rosebushes, although I couldn't be absolutely sure of that because I was looking only at the mess I'd left on the ground. And then I was gone: at about the time that the city's great fireworks display was launched, as "The Stars and Stripes Forever" was reaching its buoyant climax, I was walking swiftly along the hot, empty streets of Georgetown, feeling as if I were about to step out of one world and into another that was far less hospitable.

Trudy & Donald

late summer, 2001

Twenty-seven
[Trudy]

AUGUST IS TURNING OUT to be even worse than I'd feared. I can't remember it ever being so hot—I guess maybe I say the same thing every year—but I also can't remember feeling so dejected. I think that's because my very existence is going to change after Labor Day, when our town comes back to life and I won't, or not in the same way. For the first time, I'm not going to have that much to do and—this could just be my imagination—it's like my phone hasn't been ringing as much as it did when other summers ended.

I have to admit that Marlene DeQuella has tried to be nice. She wants me to have a farewell show right after Labor Day with some of my favorite guests and a cake with ten candles—one for every year on the air. I'm going to act totally natural and thank Marlene and the whole crew, even Pete Plantain, and pretend I'm the happiest person in the world. Then I'll tell everyone that it's like an adventure for me, a chance to do something completely different, and that for some time I've wanted to make a big change in my life. I just wish I knew what it was.

IT LOOKS LIKE we're actually staying in town for the whole month, and I can't imagine a worse way to end a rotten summer where every day there's, like, a massacre in someplace like Macedonia, and whenever you turn on the TV, there's that creepy California congressman and the missing intern, blah-blah-blah. Roger never got around to renting a place on the Vineyard or anywhere else for that matter, and he hasn't even suggested a trip to London or Paris or one of those countries we've been to a million times where no one wants to understand what you're saying and—well, I can barely stand it. I really wanted the Vineyard this year, and just about everyone I know is going to be there. Or maybe Maine. I suppose George Bush and his pals will go to Texas and put on those filthy dungarees and sweat themselves silly, which is not my idea of fun. But I'm not complaining and I try to keep my temper whenever Roger gets this blank look on his face. He really doesn't seem to care how I feel anymore and his walks at night get longer and longer.

Actually, Roger basically stopped speaking to me or anyone else after our Fourth of July party, which was such a success, and when I think about it, I realize he's been morose and almost paranoid over that break-in thing with his office. He even talked about calling the police until I reminded him that the police in this town aren't all that helpful when it comes to crime.

I wish Henrietta was alive. We may not have been all that close, but we were there for each other in a pinch and no one understood Roger better. And I have to say that I'm about to join Roger in the paranoid department after what happened the other day. I was on an errand—just going into the hot morning to buy new shoes—when I spotted Royal Arsine coming out of the Banana Republic at Wisconsin and M. "What on earth!" I muttered, and wondered what he had inside his yellow bag and how someone with such a big job had time to go shopping. "I hate that horrible man," I whispered to myself, and started to walk up the street.

But if I thought I was going to get away unseen, I was wrong. "Hey you!" Royal Arsine called out cheerfully, and I had no choice but to wait for him to catch up. The last time I'd seen him, he was all tense, but now he had this big, successful grin, which for me was even worse. When he saw me trying to peek into his shopping bag, he whispered, "Nosy, nosy!" but then he whipped out a brand-new red and blue bathing suit. As he dangled it in the hot air, the thought of him wearing it repulsed me utterly.

"Congratulations," I said, and of course he could tell I didn't mean it. I couldn't bear to look at his miniature eyes and that fluffy mustache, like a slug on his upper lip. As usual, he was wearing a dark suit with a shiny white shirt.

"No—congratulations to you," he said when we stood almost face to face and I had to look right into his pebble eyes. It was like he had known he was going to run into me.

"What do you mean?" I hated that my voice seemed to squeak.

For what seemed like a long time, we stood there in the bright heat. I thought I saw him staring at my feet, which looked a teensy bit fat in the open-toe shoes I needed to replace.

"Your husband's novel," Royal Arsine said, with this know-it-all expression. "I'll wager it's going to be a big smash."

"You're not making sense, Mr. Arsine," I said.

"Roy," he replied. "I'm talking about the book my friends in New York are talking about—how it's just going to take off. I mean, wow!" He paused and he had the strangest little smile when he added, "I think it's called *Desks of Power*. Good title."

Despite the temperature and humidity, I felt something chilly creeping up my back, and when I saw his cruel smile, I appreciated, maybe for the first time, how very clever he was at what he did.

"We have a saying where I work," he said, sounding oh-so-sophisticated with that mustache and that William Powell voice. "'What doesn't kill you seems ridiculous.'" Then he laughed, and I have to say I wasn't prepared for his laughter, which was indescribably soundless. With an extremely satisfied look, he mumbled something just as he climbed into a black Town Car that had been idling all the while by the curb. I didn't understand him at first because it sounded so French, and then I realized that what he'd said was "I'm no clef in *that* roman," just before he made a whistling noise that was probably his version of a chuckle.

AFTER THAT LITTLE ENCOUNTER, all I could think about was Roger's book, which I had tried to eject from my brain after my brief experience with its contents. I thought that if what Royal Arsine said was true—and I knew it had to be true, because he was such a manipulator—Roger's thing was coming back to distress and haunt me. And I thought how it was going to humiliate both of us for as long as we lived, that we would see people at dinner parties and they would imagine us—*me!*—doing those things he wrote about. But even while I kept wishing I had never seen those pages, I got this overpowering urge—it just wouldn't go away—to read a little bit more, if only to reassure myself that maybe it wasn't something to worry about and that I was making myself crazy for no reason. That would be easy: Roger had stopped locking his office door and it was as if he no longer cared who saw what—that he was announcing to me and everyone that he had no more secrets. Of course I still didn't want him to catch me sneaking around, so I had to be entirely sure he wasn't hiding somewhere in our big house. "Roger! Roger, sweetie!" I called, and the silence followed me right to his workroom, where I saw something on his computer screen. So it couldn't have been simpler; I pressed the print button and grabbed the pages, worrying with every whirr, with every emerging line, that Roger would come back and catch his prying wife in the act. I was so nervous by the time the printer was done that I took everything to the bathroom and locked the door.

. . . Mitch MacPeters got up from their bed and Tootsie sensed that something was wrong from the guilty way he averted his eyes and shuffled his feet and left his bathrobe undone. He had slept with Tammy Roberts, his AA, but what worried him most was the nagging fear that someone would connect him to the package he had left in the corridor outside his office, even though he had double-bagged its contents.

MacPeters remembered the ripe sweet smell of the fleecy secret fruit between the concavities of Tammy's thighs, and the separations where the smooth runway of her back, speckled with freckles, reached its end at the bend of the mysterious hillocks of her buttocks. Tootsie's back was broader than Tammy's. Her breasts were larger and her rippled nipples different, darker, in some melancholy way. As he thought about the pliant urgency of Tammy's lips, he smiled at the woman he'd married, the naïve, socially ambitious Tootsie, whose mouth, over breakfast, was filled with toast. Tootsie's lips were thicker and pinker than Tammy's, just as Tammy's were more yielding than Tootsie's. As MacPeters gobbled scrambled eggs and sausage and English muffins covered with rippling rubylike jam, the telephone rang. The senator was almost relieved when he heard the distinctive twang. "Mitch," the president said from the Oval Office. "I'm really counting on your vote to confirm my man Snike."

"I know, Mr. President, but you know my position."

"Tony Snike is a good man," the president continued. "You can't believe the things you hear, just like I can't believe those pictures of you and that good-looking Tammy lady you work with are for real. Or that cheerleader back in your home state."

MacPeters had worried about that for some time. The cheerleader had sworn to him that she was eighteen. How could he have known that she was fifteen, or that she enjoyed sexual acts that were technically illegal in most states? During the strained silence that followed, MacPeters imagined the president's familiar, moronic features—the small brow and turtlelike eyes, the supercilious mouth and thin lips. He was eager to get back to his Senate office, to taste once more the gift that his AA was so willing to offer, the honeylike warmth when his hand made its way just beneath her panty line and his engorged prick sprang out from his fly.

"Don't fuck with me, MacPeters," the president said. "Or someone's also going to hear about you—like maybe a certain Green Bay Packer."

"People will want to hear more about Tony Snike, sir," MacPeters replied, coolly, with a tight smile, controlling his rage. "I suppose you know about that dirty business with the culture minister and his twin daughters? I suppose you know what he did with that rebel leader? It was unspeakable. Who can vote to confirm a man like that?"

"This isn't some Washington novel, MacPeters," the president said, his voice rising to a crescendo of nasality, like a broken drill. "This is real life."

"In real life, I'd be telling the world the truth," MacPeters said, and he . . .

I blushed—yes, even at my age I can blush—when I dwelled on the thought that my own husband had written this, and that my good friend Donald Frizzé had read it too, every lascivious word, and I wondered again what had possessed dear Roger. *Jennifer Pouch was just going to have such a fun time with this!* I thought. *Oh, Roger!* As I shredded the pages and flushed them away—weeping the whole time—all I could think was that I had married a man I didn't know at all and that, even after all these years, I wasn't sure that I wanted to become better acquainted. I also felt increasingly annoyed with Roger for not informing me about what I had to find out from someone like the oh-so-smart Royal Arsine. It never occurred to me, not once, that Roger himself was unaware of his looming success.

Twenty-eight

❦

S O NOW THEY'VE CANCELED my farewell program because Marlene DeQuella all at once decided to do a whole
show about that slimy congressman and his disappearing intern. I
guess I can't blame her, or anyone, and maybe I would have done
the same, but it made me feel horrible and small. Suddenly it's like
I never even had a program. I guess I was feeling horrible for other
reasons too: I don't know how else to explain why, at the end of
August, I found myself kneeling on the floor of our living room,
my head resting on the cushions of our new sofa, sobbing and
sobbing, making a spectacle of myself even though I was alone. I
suppose I was crying over lots of things, like the way Roger was
acting; I can feel him slipping away from me and from everything
we've built together, and I can't stop obsessing about our friends
reading his dirty book and imagining all sorts of things about me,
even how I look naked. Does Roger think I'm the least bit like

Tootsie, with a mouth full of crumbs and sad (or did he say "sagging") yellowish boobs? One day I called my mom and I probably talked too much about myself. But she is the smartest person I know, and when she said, "Trudy, you've always had this weakness of wanting to spend time with people you don't really like very much," I had to wonder if she was right, at least partially.

I was also terribly sad about Donald Frizzé, whose wisdom and friendship mean so much to me, even when he makes me furious. I've been feeling that way since my friend Jennifer Pouch telephoned from her place in Maine to say, "I just had to give you a heads-up, Trudy, or you'd never forgive me." After Jennifer informed me that the temperature was perfect (unlike our scorching city) and the ocean warm enough for a morning swim (she had her cell phone along, so I could hear the surf) and that "I'm getting my brains fucked out" every night by someone I'd never heard of who had an extra-large penis, she told me what her newspaper was going to say: that Donald's career as a celebrity historian was built on what Jennifer called a "tissue of dishonesty." I've never been exactly sure what that phrase means—where does the tissue come in?—but I got the idea, and I wanted to believe Jennifer when she said, "And Trudy, you have to know I had *nothing* to do with it." It took me a while, but I finally telephoned Donald and told him I had to talk to him and that it was about something very important. I must have been sniffling—and he must have thought it was all about me again—because he said, "My God, Trudy, I'll be right over!" and replaced the receiver before I could say there was no great rush, although I suppose there was.

When Donald arrived, letting in a doorful of sweltering air, he looked both harried and overheated. "I came as soon as I could," he said as he kissed my cheeks, one after the other. "My car is double-parked."

I told him that nothing was wrong with me and that he certainly should park his car as one normally does.

"You made it sound like an emergency," he said a little accusingly, and wrapped me in a loose embrace.

"I don't think it's in that category," I replied, and rested my head on his broad shoulder, sniffing his masculine cologne. As I pressed against him, I thought for an instant that I detected a stirring deep inside his khakis. But it was an illusion, a sharp crease in the cotton, and there was nothing there for me. In that way, I was no different from Jennifer Pouch or, I was beginning to suspect, any woman.

"But you were crying—I heard you," Donald said, with a concerned squint that made his blue eyes briefly appear warmer and brighter. "Naturally, I was worried."

I took a half step backward. "Part of it, as I'm sure you can guess, is Roger," I said. "I love him dearly, Donald—you know that—but I can't say I know him all that well. He had a whole other life before we met—another spouse, two grown children, and government work that he's never talked about." I paused. "In the field," I added. I didn't mention Roger's nocturnal walks, which I've started to think are just to get away from me, and I certainly intended to say no more about my meaningless fling with Ricardo. Now I was sorry I'd ever mentioned it.

Donald said, "He's so much older than you too," as if he had meant to say something else.

"And then that thing he's been writing is—" I stopped because I couldn't recall if I'd ever admitted snooping around Roger's precious manuscript. "It makes me so ashamed for him!" I added.

"I'm no literary critic, Trudy," Donald said with a blink of a smile and an expression that conveyed infuriating indifference to my feelings.

Donald didn't even react when I told him the big news—that Roger's book was going to be published so that everyone in the world could read every smutty line—and I think that is because he had already guessed that my call and my tears were not about Roger but about him. I could sense that his mind was suddenly elsewhere, which I suppose was understandable, considering what I had heard from Jennifer Pouch. I wanted to be delicate about this, but when I realized that it was time to get to the point, to quiz him as a friend, the right words kept eluding me. Finally I simply told him straight out what he was facing: "They're going to call you a plagiarist, big-time," I said.

His expression didn't change, but he brushed back his buoyant hair with his left hand.

"When you say 'they,'" he said, calmly, "I wonder to whom you're referring."

"Please don't pretend," I replied, sorry to sound like a scold. But my words had their effect, and I have to say that he didn't look quite so beautiful when his features were crumpled that way. It was as if all the charm Donald possessed was disappearing right in front of me, and although he was still exceedingly handsome, he looked suddenly very ordinary and possibly a little stupid.

After several minutes, accompanied by a sniffle or two from

each of us, Donald took my right hand and held it, stroking my wrist with his thumb. I can't deny that the sensation was enjoyable, but I couldn't imagine where it would lead and was about to tell him so when he broke his silence and said, "I think my decision to drop the Hobart biography is absolutely final now."

"What biography?" I asked in what I think was a rude voice—for I had again forgotten the name of the obscure man who had historic ties to our home. Donald looked devastated by my innocent question, and it didn't seem to help when I added, "I'm so forgetful!"

"I *can't* pretend," he said then. "It's technically true. I may have borrowed a little for my book on—do you know who Levi Morton was?"

I knew that Donald had to be talking about another dead vice president.

"And also for a paper I did in college," he continued, looking earnest. "But Trudy, the word is 'borrowed'—I didn't steal anything. Phrases crept in, and so did footnotes and things like that. But it's hard sometimes to keep track—it's like you're a juggler and you have all these balls of fact going around and around in the air." He squeezed my hand as if he'd forgotten it was a hand.

"You're hurting me," I said.

"Do you believe me?"

"Of course," I replied, at just the moment I had ceased to do so.

Donald was staring at me with what I can only describe as longing.

"You're obviously wrought up," I said. "So am I—out of concern for you, naturally, and for my Roger."

Donald released my hand and bent to kiss it, but I pulled it away when I felt his tongue licking my knuckles. As he looked up, I saw a wild look in his beautiful eyes.

"I'm not very good company," I said.

"Nor am I."

He certainly wasn't, and by now I was almost angry with Donald Frizzé. When one invests in a friendship, one expects the friend to be what he claims to be—that's the minimal return, and I don't think it's wrong to expect that much. I'm sure I would have stood by Donald if he'd been sick, or poor, and of course I'll remain his friend forever. But it can't be the same, and I think Donald must have sensed what I was thinking because he looked at me with such sad eyes that I felt like crying again. I wondered if he was going to seek out his Pentagon pal, and because I was Donald's confidante, I figured I might as well just ask.

"What does Walter—Walter Listing—say?" I asked. "You never introduced him to any of us, of course."

"Oh, Trudy, Walter's such a busy man now, making policy and all that," he said, with a shake of his head. Then, in an almost distant voice, he appended, "Don't we always have to keep something of ourselves in reserve?"

"Of course," I replied, and gave Donald the embrace that he clearly craved. I pulled away only when he whispered, "I'm thinking of writing a biography of Dick Cheney—I'd be the first. What do you think?"

When I told him that it was a wonderful idea, I don't know if he thought I was being sincere. I also realized that it didn't much matter either way. Then he mumbled something I thought I heard distinctly but seemed so preposterous that I couldn't be sure.

"What did you say?" I asked when he mumbled it again.

"Bucky Ravenschlag," he said, a little impatiently.

"I beg your pardon?"

"I have to protect my reputation," he said. "Bucky will give me a forum—he admires me."

Donald, I realized only later, was prepared to cross over into a world I did not know, although since the night of our barbecue I had listened to Bucky's program, and I confess that more than once or twice I found myself wondering whether the trembling tower in Bucky's trousers was really evidence of his attraction to me. I suppose I admired the young man's innate talent, but when I thought about him for more than a moment or so, I felt a kind of shivering dread I couldn't explain.

"Did you say something?" Donald asked, retrieving my hand and clutching it.

I shook my head and tried to find words to express emotions that I couldn't begin to explain, feeling embarrassed when I started to weep in front of Donald, although in a gentle, composed way. I did sense something awful, though: in a strange blur, I felt my thrilling city, the place I had known so well for so long, falling into other hands—and imagined other hosts in other homes giving fascinating, chatty dinners with other people in the thick of things. And who was I? I asked myself. I asked that question as if I were about to disappear, to leave the landscape of my city just as surely as Woodies and Peoples Drugstore and Walter Mondale—everything in our town that had once seemed so lasting and unshakably solid.

Twenty-nine
[Donald]

❀

I T IS NOT GOING so well for me. I suppose that is something of an understatement; others would say that my life
has become a disaster area, and I'm almost certain that Jennifer
Pouch is behind it—she can be treacherous and, as Trudy once
said, "She has issues with you, Donald." But Pouch left no trail; I
know for a fact that she was in Maine when her newspaper's "literary" reporter called me and wanted to ask about what he kept
calling "some interesting overlaps" between my youthful study of
Levi Morton and the one that preceded mine by several decades.
What wounded me most was being told by this reporter person
that my mentor, G. Buster Morgenmount, had expressed "pro-
found disappointment" in me. That, he informed me, was the
exact quote.

"Right away we found maybe ten or fifteen or maybe twenty-five or fifty paragraphs that seem, like, almost word-for-word identical," the reporter said, suggesting that some sort of team had been involved in digging out this trivia. "Some ideas seemed the same too. Of course"—this he added with passive hostility—"I'm just an Average Joe reader. What do I know?"

His call had come at an awkward time. My friend Walter Listing had been over and we were on my patio, drinking morning coffee and munching muffins and marmalade, relaxing in our bathrobes as we discussed not only the concert we'd attended the night before at the Kennedy Center (they had played Ives, Brahms, and a rousing Sousa) but some preliminary goals of the new administration. Our mood was broken by this persistent telephonic intruder, and when Walter saw me shaking my head, he began to dress for work. I watched him put on his dark summer suit and cordovan bluchers, and as he knotted his silk tie, a choice blue and orange number by Hermès, I wondered, and not for the first time, why I'd never introduced Walter to my other friends. But Washington is sometimes like that; we lead partitioned lives as well as concealed ones. For instance, I knew that Walter was tasked, as he put it, with the Middle East and South Asia, and was overjoyed to be back in his old stomping ground, but I never paid much attention to his day-to-day chores across the Potomac. Also, I still worried that people might get the wrong idea about our friendship.

"Are you there?" the reporter asked, for my attention had momentarily wandered off. It's been doing that of late.

I made a real effort then to explain the situation—to assure him that my study was basically original, although, like all scholars, I relied in no small part on the work of those who had toiled before. Would someone writing about ancient Greece be accused of theft because he'd borrowed from Thucydides? I asked rhetorically. What about Rome and Suetonius—or, for that matter, Gibbon? What about Shakespeare's debt to Plutarch? I tried to make these points as forcefully as I could without being defensive or acting like an intellectual bully, but I sensed that I was losing this little battle of ideas. The subtleties of writing history are lost on some-one whose occupation consists more or less—more, actually—of taking notes. Nevertheless, I kept trying to educate my caller.

"When we write about the past," I tried to make clear, "we are constrained by what actually occurred, and by the people who ac-tually played a part. Am I making sense?"

"I'm not an idiot, Professor Frizzé," the reporter said, and for an instant I considered correcting the academic title that this idiot had bestowed. The instant passed.

"For example," I went on, "I'm deep into a biography of Garret Augustus Hobart." The moment I said that, I regretted it. Hadn't I told everyone that I'd abandoned the Hobart project? Walter List-ing, who was about to leave, gave me a puzzled glance. But now it was too late to backtrack, and so I continued, "You might ask if I'm dependent on anyone else's research, and the answer certainly is yes. How could I write about Vice President Hobart without fa-miliarizing myself with the work of our best McKinley scholars? If it was Lincoln, wouldn't I rely on Herndon—and for that matter wouldn't I rely on *other* historians who relied on Herndon? Do you see what I'm saying?"

At this point, the poor fellow was speechless; he not only seemed to have no idea how we historians go about our labors but appeared to be fairly ignorant about the turn of the last century, a period in which I was periodically immersed.

"Take Mark Hanna," I said, testing his knowledge of the era. But he surprised me by saying, "Yeah, he was like McKinley's strategy guy. So?"

I couldn't remember the point I was planning to make, but I tried to think of ways to suggest that history is more complex—and its practitioners more dependent on each other—than many lay readers realize, and said, trying to sound casual, "I suppose you think you have a little story for your big newspaper."

"I'm not exactly sure, Professor," he replied. "It's just like I said, that sometimes—actually, pretty regularly—you use the exact same turn of phrase as the other guys, if you know what I mean, and it happens so often that after a while, we sort of stopped looking. And, like, you don't seem to give much credit to anyone else."

He went on to read aloud a few sentences—my own and those penned by others—that, granted, had suspicious similarities. But a historian, I tried again to explain, is a synthesizer—someone who tries to weave together a great many strands of documentation and interpretation, of fact and speculation, of sources primary and secondary and, if need be, tertiary. If one is building a house and holds a well-made tool, why toss it out merely because you are not the first to use it?

"I'm sorry, Professor Frizzé," the reporter said, sounding, I thought, a little less assured, "but are you saying that someone else's book is like a screwdriver—something you can just pick up and use?"

"I don't believe I said that," I replied, realizing that perhaps I had said something very close to that.

My fiercely attentive interrogator was beginning to sound less like an inquiring journalist and more like a cop trying to extract a confession, as if I were prey, a suspect in a crime; but although my stomach was becoming tighter, my voice was relaxed. I could imagine precisely the pedestrian headline— "Vice Presidential Historian Accused of Plagiarism"—and how the prospect of unmasking me thrilled him. His story would undoubtedly have those damning quotations—from my work and someone else's—running parallel to the account, all underlined so that anyone could grasp what I was supposedly guilty of having done. Everyone would see it, and my pending invitation to join the Sturling Club would undoubtedly be put on hold.

"Well, my friend, you must do whatever you think you have to do," I said, trying to sound cheerful, but ready to end this fruitless dialogue. "And please let me know if I can answer any more of your questions."

"You've been very helpful," my interlocutor said, and I thought that I detected a bit of smugness in his voice, or perhaps it was triumph—sometimes it's hard to tell the difference. With that, we said our farewells, and I became nauseous, much as I had been on the Hopedales' lawn on the Fourth of July; the mere memory of those plates of pulled pork and creamy slaw only made it worse, and at that moment, it struck me, as it never had before, how all my troubles had really begun at the moment I first became involved with Trudy Hopedale. If we'd never met, I would not now feel like a condemned man, waiting for the axe, in the form of the morning newspaper, to slice me into pieces. I might never have been a semiregular on CBS, but neither would I be waiting for CBS to seal my professional doom. And logically enough I began to see this middle-aged woman with all her insularities, her questionable values, her inexcusable fibs, her vanities and pernicious cliquishness as if she were some sort of Queen Trudy. Why didn't I heed the sound advice of G. Buster Morgenmount and remain in the academy? "Hang in there, Donald," Walter Listing said, reminding me that he was still there and also that he was leaving for the day, although something in his voice suggested that he would be gone for longer than a day.

A little later, I turned on my radio and listened to Bucky Ravenschlag. He was talking about Hillary Clinton and her ambitions, but also about that sleazy congressman's troubles (far worse than mine, I consoled myself) and those murderous shark attacks, a record number, and about mice in a laboratory that never got old, if I heard correctly. He spoke of some international foe (I didn't quite get the foe's name), and he sounded not unlike Walter Listing when he declared, his voice a little higher and fiercer and faster, that we inhabit "the most awesomely powerful nation in the history of the planet Earth." Bucky's swift nasal dialogue had a way of calming me, and when he announced that he was taking calls, I lifted my telephone receiver, realizing that I had something to add to the conversation, perhaps a few words about what I envisioned was an important monograph, one that would sketch the relationship between Harry Truman and Henrietta Hopedale—a liason unfamiliar to lazy students of the presidency, such as G. Buster Morgenmount. I quickly returned the phone to its cradle, but then, a little hesitantly, I lifted it again.

Thirty
[Trudy]

❀

I CAN'T BELIEVE who called this morning: Marlene De-Quella, acting so friendly, as if she hadn't personally canceled my farewell program. It's just so *All About Eve,* and the more I think about it, the more I understand how she used her bosoms and supersweet smile to get Pete Plantain to do whatever she wanted. I'm sure Marlene was fucking Pete, or at least giving him numerous blow jobs. She was probably also doing it with the greasy-haired Allan Dood, who has gone to New York to be on cable and wear scruffy-looking costumes in foreign countries where he gets to use the word "war-torn." Anyway, Marlene's call was just incredible.

"I'm so glad I caught you," she said.

"Yes, you're very lucky," I replied. "I was just going out."

"I'm still so mad at myself, Trudy, for not having your special good-bye show. You know how we're all sometimes forced to do things that make us ashamed?"

"It doesn't matter," I assured her.

"And I was thinking anyway that I'd love to have you on at a future date as my special guest, just you and me, and we could have girl talk together. People would enjoy that."

"A wonderful idea," I said coldly, but not so coldly that she could be sure I was being cold.

"Anyway," Marlene said, "that's not why I called."

Big surprise. I knew these tricks, and I knew she had something she couldn't just come out and say like an ordinary decent person. But I have to admit I was surprised at what came next, and a little put off too.

"It's about your husband," she said. "The word is he's written a really hot book."

I didn't say anything—I was so shocked I didn't know what to say. So I waited for her to go on.

"I mean we love to have on local writers, as you know, and I just wanted to be sure we pin him down—that we're the first ones to interview the amazing Roger Hopedale. I have to tell you, Trudy, I can't wait to read it." Then she added, "I'm sure *you've* read it. Tell me what you think, just between us."

"I'm afraid you'll have to wait in line, Marlene."

"I hear it's very racy," she said, "and very excitingly told."

I WAS SO MORTIFIED and all I could think was that I wanted to protect Roger from people like Marlene, who would ask him about the sexy parts and try to make him confess that it was based on people we know. I wish Roger would get out of his slough of despondency, if that's the word, but I suppose it's partly my fault for nagging him all through August about having to stay in town, and of course he is a little puzzled by what's happened, all the attention he's suddenly getting. "You know, I can't recall actually submitting my manuscript to a publisher," he said with a completely baffled expression when he first heard. But he never said anything about withdrawing the book, which he would have had every right to do. He won't admit it, at least not to me, but I know he is absolutely thrilled about his prospects, and he just gets angry when I say that even though I haven't read a word (which he doesn't believe) the whole business makes me very, very nervous. And he gets even more annoyed when I tell him how it might end badly and that what he really ought to do is go back to what he knows, like American supremacy and all that. The last time I said it, he became all stiff and superdignified, almost like he was when I met him years ago at that Senate hearing, but instead of flirting and being sweet the way he was then, he began to lecture me about literature, which he somehow pronounced with five syllables. In the most pompous way, he said, "My expertise will certainly make its way into my art," and then he called me "inane." But if anyone in our household is inane, it's Roger. If I told him that Royal Arsine was behind it and wanted to embarrass him, he would have yelled at me.

This episode has been especially distressing, because Roger, despite his flaws, really does mean the world to me. (I don't think this is the place to get into more of those flaws.) And he's such an honorable person. When we saw the story about Donald Frizzé, we were in our spacious kitchen quietly having breakfast; Roger was nibbling on his crumbly toast and pointed at the headline that said, "Plagiarism Charges Bedevil Historian." I tried to grab the section away, but Roger was determined to finish the article, which he read with his head shaking from left to right, his dark nostrils eyeing me. With every wobble of Roger's head, I felt so very sorry for this person who had been my friend. I knew that it had to be totally devastating.

Of course I had expected this ever since I got that telephone call from my friend Jennifer Pouch, but still: seeing your life's work turned to rubble has to be awful, and several times that morning I almost called Donald to ask how he was holding up. In the end, though, I didn't call, because I wasn't exactly sure what I would say. Also, Roger's advice was to see how things developed over the next few days. He pointed out that no one had been as loyal to Donald as the Hopedales and that if anyone ought to telephone anyone, Donald ought to call us and apologize for letting everyone down. My head could see he was right, but my heart made me want to pick up the phone anyway.

I know that Roger has always had very mixed feelings about Donald, but it's also becoming clear that Roger has mixed feelings about me; sometimes, like when he called me "inane," it's like he regards me as an inferior being, a foolish person incapable of seeing the world with his wise perspective. Sometimes I almost think he doesn't like me anymore, as if he's angry about something he won't talk about. One late night—he was muttering in his sleep—I heard him say, "We can't go on," and I could have sworn he said "Tootsie," which really hurt my feelings. I also have to admit that I shudder when Roger touches me in certain ways; it's like he's taking notes or something, although there's been a lot less of that lately; in that department, he is pretty much retired.

A day or so after that story about Donald, I went to a cocktail party at Jennifer Pouch's place—I felt I had to be there—and Jennifer was a little hard to take, looking so smug and suntanned as she circled around her little apartment and introduced everyone to the man she's been seeing, the one with the great big penis, who can't be more than thirty. I knew most of the people there, and I guessed that the others were journalist types that Jennifer had to invite, and I was so glad Roger didn't want to come; it was all a little depressing to be swallowing warm cheese squares and white wine and to hear people talking about poor Donald Frizzé as if he had died or something. I really didn't want to talk to anyone, especially not Jennifer's new boyfriend, who looked incredibly fit and, if you ask me, incredibly boring.

Just as I was leaving, the elevator door opened and there was Royal Arsine, along with some skinny man with a crew cut and a plug in his ear. "Trudy Hopedale, you can't go yet," he said, almost like a command but smiling, and so, against my better judgment, I went back inside and watched everyone fall just about silent at the sight of the new guest, whose face they recognized from the confirmation hearings. Jennifer almost literally flew over to him and gave him a familiar peck on his cheek, right next to his little mustache.

I didn't talk for long to Roy, as he still insisted I call him despite his fancy new title, but I'll admit it wasn't all that unpleasant. "I intend to have a long and happy career in this town," he said. Roy certainly does have a career now and—I hate to say it— I understand that he's quite a prize at dinner parties because he's an extra man (or at least no one's ever seen a wife). Also, I could finally see how he can be quite funny and charming when he's able to relax and just be himself, the way he was at Jennifer's place, which turned out to be a really fun and interesting evening. So I'm glad I stayed for another hour or so. Of course Roy is awfully full of himself, and he managed to let everyone know that he personally briefs the president or at least someone who is close to the president. I don't know what he briefs them *about* and I doubt that Roy would tell me, although he has a teensy little crush on me and so he might say something if I pushed. But no matter what—and I can see how other people might find him magnetic—he gives me the willies. "It's amazing, the difference between being inside the teepee and being out," he said, and one of his little stony eyes started to blink when he added, in that oh-so-sophisticated voice, "I imagine that being out is a little rough for my old pal Roger now." Then, with a terrible giggle, the kind that made his bristly mustache shake, he said, "But it will probably get worse when his—what's the word? his *tome?*—is sprung on the world." I wouldn't let Roy get my goat, and so, with as big a smile as I could muster, I said, "I have to wonder, Roy, if it's a little bit about you." But then he said, "Maybe it's a little bit about Roger too," and after that, he only giggled again and I went to talk to someone less important.

Thirty-one

✿

I WOULD NEVER DROP Donald Frizzé as a friend, and it was only when I heard him on the radio with Bucky Ravenschlag—talking so millions of people could hear—that I decided we could no longer be the sort of friends we had been. I understand why Donald did it, and I suppose I can forgive him personally. People need to preserve their standing in this town. But your standing is not the worst thing you can lose, if I'm making any sense. That's exactly what I said to Jennifer Pouch after Labor Day when I saw her at a big black-tie benefit for some rare disease that afflicts the nephew of a person we all know.

For the first time, Roger and I sat at one of the outer tables, next to people we'd never met—people who had paid top dollar for their tickets and seemed to be a little too impressed by who was there, local television celebrities like Marlene DeQuella, who looked slutty in her short skirt, but mainly bigwigs from Congress and the administration. Marlene gave me a big hug and a cheek kiss, which was the picture that ended up in the Style section, with a caption that said "Embraceable You." I hated that photograph. I couldn't believe my own facial expression, or how I got that droopy flap under my chin, and I only hope people didn't recognize me. Of course Marlene basically ignored me and pushed her boobs into Roger's face and may have gotten him to promise he'd be on her show when his book came out, which made me just shudder. "*Desks of Power* is such a wonderful title!" I heard her exclaim, and Roger, although he had barely said a word to me— nothing new in that—suddenly became very talkative and just couldn't take his eyes off the declension at the top of Marlene's skimpy blouse. There was also this horribly uncomfortable moment when Ricardo Willingham came over to our table and kissed my cheek and put out his hand to Roger, who looked away from the senator as if he hadn't seen him or his hand. When it dawned on me that Roger had to know all about Ricardo and must have decided to forgive me, I felt horribly ashamed and almost cried right then and there. A moment later, I leaned over and hugged Roger, but he didn't seem to notice.

The one really strange encounter I had that night was with someone I ought to have known but had never managed to meet—Donald's friend Walter Listing, who has been in the news because of his job, which is at least as huge as Royal Arsine's job. Walter Listing had a seat at a front table because he's so influential and also because he knows a person whose son actually has that horrible rare disease we were celebrating and raising money for. I have to say that he made me uncomfortable, the way he rolled his eyes and moved his lips like he was about to mock me whenever I opened my mouth. He also had this fluttery patronizing smile and kept saying, "Trudy, Trudy," as if I was some silly person. I tried to imagine what sort of guest he'd make at one of our dinners.

Roger told me once that Walter Listing is responsible for lots of fascinating ideas about fighting new kinds of wars, but there's nothing warlike about him when you see him in his dinner jacket, which makes his face look redder and his hair whiter. He has these soft little hands and puffy short lips, and you have to wonder what it would be like to kiss him. He's one of those people who could be just about any age, and even though he must be close to seventy, it doesn't look like he has a beard, not the way he pours talcum powder all over his face. I know I'm rambling, but the point is that Walter Listing had never spoken to me before, and at this benefit dinner, while the speakers were droning on about that hideous disease, which made all of us feel so lucky not to have it, he made his way back to our table, like he knew who I was, and after he nodded to Roger, who looked very sulky, he said, "Our Donald will have to keep a low profile for a while, I'm afraid, until this blows over." People close by recognized Walter Listing and seemed to be quite impressed that he had sought me out.

"Do you think it *will* blow over?" I heard myself asking, as if Walter and I were old friends. "It sort of goes to the core of who he is, doesn't it?"

"Trudy, Trudy, we're seldom who we are," he replied with a knowing glance at Roger, and even though that didn't make a lot of sense at the time, it started to when I heard Donald on the radio telling Bucky Ravenschlag that he had never liked being in Washington anyway, and maybe he had taken shortcuts in his work, but he'd always tried to live a principled life, and he'd never looked down on anyone like certain people did. Then—and I couldn't believe this even though I heard it with my own ears—Donald mentioned my name. "I adore Trudy Hopedale," he told Bucky and four million strangers, "but she represents a lot that's wrong with this town. Trudy Hopedale and her fancy circle think they know it all and that's all there is to know. I can tell you, speaking as an historian, that no one ever knows it all. Or not for long"—at which point Donald actually mentioned that he was going to write about poor Henrietta's nutty Truman fantasy (I still can't believe I heard it right, but I did), which will make it even harder for me to forgive him. After Bucky said, "You're a brave man for coming on and telling the truth," I thought for a minute about calling in myself. Then I shut off the radio and left it shut off.

ANYWAY, I'M TRYING to look ahead, because it's September and the season is about to get cranked up and it's actually a relief not to have to do my tiresome program anymore. Maybe I'll do something completely different, like teaching poor children to read or volunteering at a soup kitchen on Fourteenth Street, where all those men in torn shoes line up, or at least something more meaningful than talking to people who are just so full of themselves.

At least the Clintons and their cronies are gone. Our city changes all the time—it's exciting to watch it up close, even though it's hard to see what George W. Bush wants to accomplish despite all his talk about education and cutting taxes and how he's against growing human beings for spare body parts. Everyone who knows him personally thinks he's really smart and charming, not at all like he acts on television when he tries to express his thoughts, and I'd like to do more to welcome him and his friends to our town. I'd love to start planning a really huge party and cover the table with late-summer flowers and that new china we ordered from England, although I can't do it all alone. I'll have to wait until Roger gets back from wherever he's gone. Even though he's been in bad spirits—I know he's worried sick about his book, as if it's just dawned on him that people will read it—I never thought he would vanish without warning. At first I thought he was playing a game and hiding in his workroom, but in the late afternoon, when it was time to begin thinking about a meal (I wanted to try that Albanian restaurant in Adams Morgan that Jennifer Pouch had raved about), I knew right away that something was amiss. For one thing, the door to his little office was wide open, and when I stepped inside for a closer look, I saw a note: "Trudy, I'm going to be away, perhaps for some time. R." Also, drawers were open, his computer was gone, and the place looked as if it had been totally cleaned out. Only a few scraps of paper remained, on one of which I saw typing, and then the phrase "Mitch nibbled the nubs of Tootsie's mottled nipples." In a fury, I shredded that into confetti. "Oh, Roger," I murmured to myself, and when I saw that the closet in our bedroom was half empty, I realized that for reasons unbeknownst to me, he had decided to move out.

I was probably close to tears the next day when Jennifer Pouch called. In the telephonic distance, she sounded sweet, just like a real friend. "How *are* you?" she asked. "Busy, I imagine, what with all the changes in your life." I told her that she imagined right, and that all was just perfect.

The silence that followed my declaration was a signal that she was after information, and finally she came out with it and said, "I hear he's left you."

Although Jennifer has been a dear friend for some time, I thought this was rude and inappropriate.

"Jennifer, I can tell you that Roger isn't here, but I don't think you can say he 'left me,' or anything like that. As far as I know, he's out for a walk, although perhaps a long one." I paused for a moment, imagining how this was sounding. "Don't you *dare* tell anyone that Roger has left me, and anyway it's not *me* that he left."

I wish Roger was here because summer will be over soon and it gets darker more quickly every day, and when he's gone I always worry that something will happen to him and I'll have to spend the rest of my days alone in our big house. I can't bear that idea, no matter how many happy memories I have, and when the telephone rang a day or so later, which I hoped was Roger, it was only Gail Tachyon on the line, telling me in that syrupy voice of hers how much we could get for our historic home. I didn't feel angry, probably because I never thought of her as a friend in the first place.

I hope Roger knows how much I genuinely care for him, and I hope that he can permanently forgive me for anything I might have done to hurt him. I understand how self-centered I can act, but sometimes it's like I'm trying to catch up with myself, like I'm on a carousel or something, spinning, and that every time I come around, I hope I'll arrive at something new. That's what makes me keep looking ahead, to imagine the fun of having different people at our next party, maybe Walter Listing or even someone like Bucky Ravenschlag, though I don't like it when Bucky talks about "flexing our power" and "eating our enemies alive." But I appreciate his good qualities, like the way he's overcome his immense handicap, and of course Roger still knows lots of people who used to work for the president's father and maybe we could have some of them over too—everyone knows how special an evening at the Hopedales' is—and naturally we wouldn't want to leave out our older friends. I hope that even Donald Frizzé will be a guest again someday, when people forget his mistakes; everyone always does in this town, or at least they say they do; or I hope so. It's hard for people who don't live here to understand any of this or to truly know ordinary people like me who find themselves in the vortex of history and destiny. That's what lets us put our differences behind us and brings us together so that we can talk about and even celebrate the things we'll always have in common.

About the Author

Jeffrey Frank, a native of Washington, is a senior editor at *The New Yorker*. He lives in Manhattan with his wife, Diana.